to Laura

You're never late, you're
on the right kind of time.
Let's swap stories ♡

Claire

I'VE NEVER DONE THIS BEFORE

Entering each chapter became for me...*an induction into another's reality*: a glimpse of another's pain, joy, ambivalence, fear, lust, and...humanity.

—Daniel Maurer / Author, *Sobriety: A Graphic Novel*

I've Never Done This Before is solid proof of the adage that bad decisions make for great stories. It's full of startling, damaging actions, made without forethought or foresight, that tear a reader along through their thrills and misapprehensions. Better yet, the writing here, in its subtlety and insight, often delivers the more lasting, resonant pleasures of lessons learned, and the possibility of brighter futures.

—Peter Rock / Author, *My Abandonment*

Foster's prose is vivid and sharp, carving out absurd and brutal stories that will make you ache. *I've Never Done This Before* is painful in the best possible way.

—P.E. Garcia / Editor, *Hunger Mountain: VCFA Jounal of the Arts*

Each voice is uniquely, fantastically hers. And perfectly theirs. And ultimately, ours.

—Matt Glarner / Co-Host, *Since Right Now Addiction Recovery Podcast*

I'VENEVERDONETHISBEFORE

by

Claire Rudy Foster

‡

Printed in the United States of America

First Printing, 2016

ISBN 978-0-9980727-0-8

Illustrations by Aaron Lee Perry

Design/Layout by C. Lorin Aguirre

Another KLĒN + SŌBR Intervention™

PO Box 440401

Saint Louis, MO 63144

This one's for The Dude and Lewis Jones.

‡

X

‡

WRITE SOBER, EDIT SOBER

I fell in love with writing when I was about 8 or 9 years old.

My parents took a subscription to the *New Yorker*, which was in its heyday for fiction: Alice Munro, Louise Erdrich, Stephen King, David Foster Wallace, and George Saunders graced its pages. I leafed through each issue greedily, studying the cartoons before I turned to the short story.

At the time, it was like reading a foreign language. I was already a voracious consumer of words. I couldn't leave the library without at least five or six paperbacks. I had a running tab of overdue fines, which I paid out of my allowance. Between library visits I picked at my parents' bookshelves, choosing novels by Alice Hoffman and Laurie Colwin. I read few children's books, preferring survival manuals.

This strange, new, short fiction bewitched me.

First, it was about grownups. They got drunk, used forbidden swears, and rubbed each other the wrong way. They were complicated animals. Second, I didn't completely understand what I was reading, which didn't slow me down at all. I dissected those stories the way some kids take apart a pocket watch, trying to figure out how it ticked. I was hooked. And then I started to try to write my own stories, with the concentration of a junkie learning to make her own dope.

I admit to copying, liberally and shamelessly, every author whose work I enjoyed. Over the years I imitated Robin McKinley, Lydia Davis, Zadie Smith, and many others. My taste was eclectic, so I mimicked everything. Genre fiction as well, from Isaac Asimov and Ray Bradbury, down the line to Danielle Steele and Mercedes Lackey. By the time I finished college I was an accomplished copyist, and had gotten enough confidence to start putting my writing out for publication in the journals.

By then, I also had a serious problem with alcohol and drugs.

For me, being fucked up gave me the same excellent feeling as a reading a good novel. Drugs engrossed me, bewildered me. They changed the story in my head. Instead of feeling like a sore thumb, a freak, a geek, I felt *cool*. I was fucking cool. I wore sunglasses all the time, telling myself that they were like bulletproof glass, separating me from the rest of the world. I smoked unfiltered Luckys through a black cigarette holder. I let myself be weird. I was a character; my life was the plot.

When I drank, my insecurity about my writing—was I actually any good?—subsided. I was part of a long, sodden tradition. I was on the same continuum as F. Scott Fitzgerald, Hunter S. Thompson, Irvine Welsh, and William Faulkner. I copied their prose and their habits, hoping to induce the same creative effects in myself. (I didn't know then that one of my favorites, David Foster Wallace, got sober before producing some of his finest work.)

At the time, I believed that getting drunk had to be part of the creative process. Write drunk, edit sober? I wrote drunk, edited on speedballs. My benders lasted for days, and I produced increasingly bizarre, disjointed stories. I told myself that these were "experimental fiction," that I was really on to something. Once, on a speed-fueled jag, I filled an entire Moleskine notebook. I ran through four ballpoint pens in one night. My handwriting looked like glossy stick bugs marching across the page. My hand cramped so badly that I couldn't light my own cigarettes. I remember that those stories made *perfect sense* at the time, and the words came out of me in a swarm. Writing like this was intoxicating, and I never, ever wanted it to end.

Unfortunately, my muse ran out around the same time my tolerance leveled up. Suddenly, it took me much longer to get into the magic, morphine-clouded space where I thought my best stories hovered. Speed, weed, heroin, cocaine, and alcohol were my lockpicks, and I applied them night after night to the door, hoping to enter the magic kingdom.

Waking up the next morning, I'd look over my pages and wonder, who the fuck wrote this? Who the fuck wants to read this?

At the time, I was consuming two bottles of champagne a day, two joints, an incalculable amount of cocaine, and a smattering of evening cocktails. I took prescription morphine, which was cleaner than the absinthe and homemade laudanum I had favored in college. My drug use wasn't self-indulgent, I told myself. It was for work: I was trying to write a novel. I worked on the draft every day, even though it wasn't exactly a fun thing to do. Long fiction made me look at myself, hard. It wasn't clever, the way my short fiction was. It showed me my weaknesses. I was young, I wasn't any good, I was working on my own. But writing was the only thing I had going for me—so, by God, I was going to write.

Every day was exactly the same for me. I was by some miracle managing to hold down a day job—I was a virtual receptionist on the early day shift, clocking in at 5 a.m. and leaving at 1:30. I showed up on time every morning, still drunk from the night before. My hangover started to prick me around noon, so on the way home I stopped by one of the three or four stores that I rotated through, bought two bottles of wine, and went home. Every day I came home, rolled a joint, put a towel under the door, and wrote with an open bottle of champagne next to me. An hour or two in, I'd take a pill and feel myself melt into the chair. I didn't think. I just wrote. I wrote until I passed out, and then I woke up, drank some more, and went out to the bars to see people. I'd get home around 3 a.m., sleep for an hour, and then go to my job.

Rinse and repeat. At the end, I hallucinated while I was awake; I was never not loaded. I was always sick. I was physically unable to get high and mentally incapable of concentrating on my novel. That was the kicker: I couldn't fucking write.

———

Sober, the part of my mind that naturally seemed to fill up with stories was inaccessible to me.

The door, locked; no keys, no hairpins, no way to force my way in. The insecurity that rattled me every time I sat down to work was even louder than before. For the first six months, I gave up completely. I concentrated on getting healthy, learning to live without using daily. My ability to form coherent sentences eventually returned, but for a long time I wasn't able to read. My brain just didn't work. Words came back to me slowly, and I was afraid to try writing.

At the end of that year, moving to a new apartment, I found a stack of paper in the back of a closet, with a rubber band around it. It was the draft I'd worked on every day in the last days of my drinking. It wasn't finished, just a 200-page manuscript in progress. I took it out with shaking hands. Was it any good? I sat down in the closet and started to read what I'd written. Part of me hoped that it would be brilliant, or at the very least good enough to justify the amount of booze I'd poured myself to get those words on paper. I was looking for proof that I was becoming the writer I wanted to be, that my efforts were bearing fruit. More than anything, I wanted reassurance that it hadn't all been for nothing—that I'd made something beautiful in spite of myself. Something worth saving.

About a quarter of the way into the manuscript, I started checking page numbers. Flipped forward, then back. They were in order, but the text on the page was repetitive. My main character had, of course, poured himself a drink and was getting ready to fall down the stairs. I spent ten pages describing his Victrola—converted into a liquor cabinet, naturally. And then walked him to the top of the stairs and placed his hand on the banister. In the novel, he was going to miss the first step and slide all the way to the bottom on his face. I read the scene, turned the page, and read the scene again. On the next page, the same scene, with slightly different details. The whole manuscript was like this—loops and loops of repeating text.

I realized why. Every day, I sat down, got high, and got to work—and wrote the same scene over again. I had no memory of what I'd written the day before, so every sentence felt new, like progress, when in reality I was just going in circles. I was crushed. All of that time, dedication, and effort had been wasted.

The blow to my ego was the worst part. For years I'd styled myself as a writer: Sylvia Plath in Doc Martens. I loved showing off my writerlyness. When someone commented on it, I basked in the attention. I found subtle ways to brag about my discipline, what I'd read, my highbrow subjects, my few small successes. Here's the fantasy: someone finds my writing after my death and is astounded by my deep sensitivity, my tragically unacknowledged gift. If I'd died in that apartment—and I overdosed more than once, and drank myself sick—I would have nothing to show for it. Just trash. Cleverly worded trash. I imagined someone holding up a story I'd written, examining it, and sadly shaking his head. "She was so young," he'd say. "And so untalented."

What really burned me was that in spite of how badly I wanted to be a real writer, all I'd managed to produce was a haystack of worthless pages. I threw the draft away, finished packing, and told myself that it was time to make some changes.

———

I was almost two years sober when I sat down to write again.

In the meantime, I read a lot, drank coffee, and pushed a few sentences around. But nothing grabbed me. The sense of being inspired—finding my muse at the end of a rail of cocaine—wasn't there. I went to AA meetings and listened to other people's stories. "I should be writing this down," I thought to myself. But I didn't.

My problem with drinking was that it made it impossible for me to separate the process from the product. I couldn't write while sober, and I couldn't create while drunk. My lack of perspective kept me going in circles. My image of myself as a writer let me justify my behavior. I'd poured fuel on the fire in the name of my art. But I had to come to terms with the fact that I wasn't that good, drunk or sober. And if I'd kept going, I would have ended up killing myself. To be honest, if that manuscript I found in the closet had been as good as I was hoping, I would have gone right back into my old rituals. But it *wasn't*. I had to find a new way. Slowly, one day at a time, I built a regular routine and got working again.

These days, I write sober and edit sober. I try to be humble about my writing, with mixed results. Writing while not under the influence has shown me my shortcomings—and recovery gave me the ability to work on them, instead of huffily defending them as part of my style. I can see my improvement over the last few years. I know I'm not going in circles. Best of all, I don't need alcohol or drugs to get into the creative part of my mind or to see myself as a creative person. I keep putting in the work. At the end of the day, I have something to show for it.

Am I brilliant? Probably not. Writing sober, I can say: not now. Not *yet*.

X

STORIES

‡

I

CHINOOK

Betsy and her husband Dave drove south to Coos Bay at the beginning of chinook season, their Volvo packed with empty coolers and an industrial scale. Betsy dozed with her head against the window, half-listening to Dave argue with the radio.

"What crap," he muttered, thumbing the volume up. "As if the executives gave a damn about the environment." He would talk this way whether Betsy was asleep or not—sometimes his voice spilled like oil through her dreams, and she would wake up with the sense that he'd followed her through the many rooms in her head.

It was the week after their fifth wedding anniversary—the drive to Coos Bay both a favor for some friends, who owned a restaurant in Portland, and a second honeymoon. The first one had been the cap on their fairy tale wedding, a getaway that was no internet and all Hawaiian sunsets. Betsy remembered the scent of the orchid in her hair. Dave was still willing to dance with her then, and their skin was tan from naps on the beach. Their faces hurt from smiling. She'd been so sure they were going to make it.

This trip was different. Five unhappy years stretched tight between them. Dave had taken off a week from work, withdrawn a slim stack of twenties from their bank account.

"Do you have the directions?" he asked Betsy, though the map lay open in her lap.

She stirred, rubbed her hand over the pink spot on her cheek. "Just a minute." The lines on the paper, too many colors, numbers written like black ants. "Where are we?"

"You're supposed to be the navigator."

She picked up the map, brought it close to her face. "I was resting." She ignored his exasperated sigh, the way he brought his finger down precisely at their coordinates. He turned up the radio another click, rolled down the windows. She closed her eyes again, letting the rush of summer air make clots of her hair, strands adhering to her face like struggling flies.

Their friends Sam and Kate had a cabin near Coos Bay, up the hill from the bay itself with a view of the rusting docks and clusters of old boats. The restaurant's success had bought the cabin, and the three cliff-side acres of pines that wrapped around it. In the hall, sliding off her sandals, Betsy put her hand on the wall to steady herself. Beside her splayed fingers, a framed photograph of Sam and Kate side-by-side in their kitchen, in matching white aprons, grinning at the camera while their hands dug through a trench of fresh field greens. They couldn't find time to visit Coos Bay now—too busy—but they'd handed over the key on a ribbon, and asked for a couple hundred pounds of chinook. *If it's not too much trouble,* they had said, handing Betsy a blank check. *See what you can get for us?* As though she knew how to negotiate, knew a salmon from a snapper. But the opportunity to get away, to spend some time with Dave—to fix, maybe, whatever needed fixing—was too tempting.

She missed being close to him. She blamed his job, the mandatory immersion in programmer culture, but there was more to it. He turned away from her now, in bed. Or was limp when she reached for him. She often caught him late at night, looking at luminous, perverse bodies on the computer's glowing screen. Betsy didn't look like those women. She didn't like doing the things they did, had nearly been sick when Dave tried to get her to go through the motions. *Do it for me, babe.* She couldn't tell any of this to Kate, who had been her maid of honor and was so happy that it felt like a personal insult. She'd slipped her friends' check into her purse alongside the key, accepted Kate's dry kiss and the highlighted map.

In the bedroom, she heard Dave drop the suitcases on the thin carpet. Then, the zipper of his computer case. "No wireless," he called. She shrugged, though he couldn't see her, and went into the small kitchen. The window over the sink looked out on the bay, a rusty inlet where the river met the sea and the discolored coats bobbed at the wharf as though nursing. A few sails dotted the harbor, specks against the blue-soup water. Betsy tried to imagine what it would be like to be out on the water, squinting as the sun slapped down. The bay bridge loomed on its pilings, casting long shadows on the ribbons of kelp shimmering just beneath the surface.

Dave appeared behind her, opened the fridge. "Only one beer," he said, cracking open the can. "We should make a run to the store tonight."

"I'm tired of being in the car." She didn't take her eyes off the bay. She heard him swallowing, then the can collapsing in his grip.

"Just me, then. It's not even four, there's time."

Betsy turned on the water, put her fingers under the faucet. Her skin seemed very white, her nails nearly purple in the cold water. "Ask where to get the fish," she said. "Ask the cashier."

He kissed her cheek, yeasty breath in her ear. "See what you can find to eat."

‡

Sam and Kate, of course, had a stash of pasta in the cabinet—orzo, rigatoni, all different shapes, as though they'd planned a dinner party. The freezer held a pair of steaks, wrapped in plastic and foil, and under the sink Betsy found a row of jars, each stuffed with vegetables. She held them up to the light, eyeing the murky beans and rings of squash. Pickles, suspended in brine like organs. She chose the tomatoes, leaking pink and pips into a thick silt at the bottom of the jar, and tapped the Mason ring gently on the edge of the counter. The suction released in a loud pop, and the kitchen filled with the last-summer scent of cooked vegetables. She salted a pot of water and put it on the gas burner, turned up high. The window let in a square patch of sun that idled across the ceiling. Betsy leaned against the counter, arms crossed, watching it waver over the white paint.

Dave came back late, with two paper sacks of groceries and a rack of cheap beer. He set the bags on the small dining table and flopped into one of the Shaker chairs.

"Sorry I'm late," he said. "Did you cook? It's nice in here."

She brought him a bowl of pasta, the sauce thick and topped with a handful of toasted pine-nuts. "No pepper."

"Other people's houses," he said, and smiled as she handed him a fork. "Would you hand me a beer?"

She opened it for him, set it by his elbow. They were on vacation, after all. He'd want to drink, and sleep in late. He'd taken long shifts at the office, more programming projects, hours staring into the computer's screen. He'd say he deserved a break—from everything, from cooking, from the obligations of a honeymoon. He might sneak away to "relax" with his computer. Live chatting or real time gaming. She watched him eat, feeling merciless. When the pasta slid off his fork, she frowned and went to stand by the stove, white ceramic spattered with tomato.

"Did you unpack?" she asked.

"Just the laptop. There's a dresser, if you want." The noodles slithered in the bowl, leaving flecks of olive oil on the table. His chewing seemed too loud, indecent. She glared at him, and when he didn't look up, clanged the knives and spoons against one another in the sink, scraping and rinsing a little too loudly.

"I'm going for a walk," she said when she was done.

"You alright?"

"I'll be back later." She paused in the doorway. "Did you ask about the fish?"

"Forgot." He eyed the pot on the stove. "Any more of this? It's good."

She was already gone.

The path down to the beach was steep and fairly rough—she slid sideways in her sandals, tearing up a gritty handful of weeds to slow herself. The yellow dust coated her toes. A lizard eyed her from the shade of a small bush, winking when she passed. The day was still hot, although it was nearly dusk. She felt her shoulders start to burn, even in the last light— Portland had been rainy for weeks, and she'd forgotten sunscreen. She slid again, running her palms over the sandy soil.

"Goddammit," she hissed. The beach, a thin strip of stones, glimmered twenty feet below her. Most likely, if she fell, Dave wouldn't hear her screaming. He'd be plugged into his computer, hacking away at some troll army, jerking off, sipping beer. If she broke her leg, or sprained her wrist even, she wouldn't be able to make it back up the cliff. *How selfish he is*, she thought, as her sandals touched the shore's lip. The water lapped over her toes, smudging off the dirt. Looking over her shoulder, she saw that it wasn't a long descent. There was a substantial streak in the dirt where she'd slipped. The lizard, no doubt, was laughing at her. She squatted down, took a handful of loose gravel, picked through it for sea glass.

There were salmon crowding the bay, she knew it. Sam and Kate would have loaded the coolers together, brushing shoulders, laughing. So sure of themselves. A team. They would have edged down the cliff together, holding hands. Skipped stones over the weak, close waves.

☨

The next morning, Betsy took the car keys and drove down to the little convenience store—Dave had forgotten both eggs and coffee. She lingered in the candy aisle, adding a little bag of peanut brittle and a can of chips, things she would never eat at home.

"Is that all?" the cashier asked, taking her folded twenty. "There's better coffee down the street, you know. None of this Folgers stuff."

"It's fine," Betsy said. She watched him open the paper bag, as though unfolding a sheet for surgery. He put the coffee in, painstakingly slipped a rubber band around the carton of eggs. "Can I ask you something?"

"You need directions?"

"I'm looking to buy some chinook." She smiled, trying to look like the kind of woman who did this all the time. "Do you know anyone?"

"How much do you need?"

"A few hundred. Pounds, not fish. I have coolers," she said. He looked past her, as though checking her car, then nodded.

"You need to go see Tyee. He does small-supply stuff, lives down by the wharf."

She was already taking a pen from her bag, ready to scribble on her receipt. "Thank you," she said. "What's his address? Tyee?"

The cashier laughed, showing a capped gold molar. "*Address.* That's funny. You go down by the wharf and turn left at Sambo's. His house is the red one. Got a few buoys hanging up, maybe a dog out front. You can't miss it."

"The red house," she repeated, writing the directions down anyway. "Thank you. Is he a friend of yours?"

This time, the cashier only grinned. "Not my kind," he said, and handed her the bag of groceries. "Have a nice day, now."

In the car, she dialed Dave's cell phone but got no answer. "I got a lead on some fish," she told his voicemail. "I know we've got a couple days, but I thought I'd see what's out there. There's peanut butter and toast in the kitchen for breakfast, okay? Call me later." She hung up, certain that he'd gone back to sleep. Or was in his favorite spot, locked in the bathroom with the light off, his private place for watching.

Mid-week meant no tourists on the boardwalk, the shops opening later, their neon dimmed. *Closed Til Friday.* Betsy drove along the water, inhaling the slightly rotten breeze that was puffing off the bay. The white pilings shrank, becoming discolored as she got away from the esplanade, breaking like uneven bones. Even their copper caps disappeared. A seagull standing on one foot turned its face away from her, dropping a yellowish turd onto the soggy wood. The boats, too, seemed to relax at their moorings—the wood carrying the tide's salt handprints, lines of green scum dribbling like necklaces at their bows. A man stood on the deck of the *Sturgeon's Daughter*, holding an empty crab trap. He waved to Betsy, and she raised her hand in return.

The house where Tyee lived was a shed, smaller than she'd expected. A rusted bicycle frame lay by the cement-block porch, its warped wheels stacked on the ground beside it. The mailbox was a dented coffee can with a tin flap nailed over its mouth, the name *Black* painted in neat blue letters over the dimpled metal. There was no dog, but she saw a rope hitched to a car tire, a chewed tennis ball, a tuft of silver hair in a crack of wood. She knocked on the splintery door, waited.

"Are you Tyee?" she asked the man. He was Indian, high cheekbones, already scowling. "I'm sorry, someone gave me your name."

"What time is it?" he asked, glancing at the sun.

"Nine. Or ten. Is it too early? I can come back." His shirt was ragged, and the arm that rested on the door frame covered in black tattoos—a jumping whale, an eagle with a salmon in its claws.

He sighed, looked over his shoulder. "Stay," he said, and she wondered for a moment if it was a dog or a woman in the house.

He didn't ask if she minded, but lit a cigarette anyway and stepped out onto the porch. He was tall, and she saw that the tattoos completely covered both arms, even peeking out from his collar. The words *Alaska Pride* inked on his neck, a fin reaching up to touch the curling letters.

"I heard you sell salmon," she said. Crossed her arms. She felt pale, her skin prickling as he scanned her with his brown eyes. "Chinook?"

"I have fish," he said. Blew a plume of smoke. "I'm not Tyee, though. I'm Simon. The other one is a nickname."

She nodded, as though she understood.

He tapped the ash from the end of the cigarette, inspected the glowing tip. "Tyee is a dead man. A dead king. How much fish you need?"

"A few coolers. I have them in the car."

"You have money?"

She nodded. "I could pay you today, if you'll take a check." She realized that she had no idea how much chinook cost—she couldn't bargain without seeming ignorant. And it was Sam and Kate's money, not her own. What if she paid too much?

"Check, huh. This look like a bank?" But he smiled, stubbed out the filter, and led her behind the shack to a pair of dented freezers under an aluminum awning. Someone had taken a crowbar to one of the locks—she could see where the black teeth had gouged the white steel. There was a pile of rope, coils of red and yellow twine, a green pole net. He kicked a rusty-looking float aside, took a key on a slim silver chain from his pocket.

"These are fresh," he said, lifting the lid like a coffin. She peered down. Packed in chipped ice, the chinook gaped up at her, their eyes large and jellyish, fins frozen to their sides. "I'll get more like this today, tomorrow too."

"How fresh?" She reached into the ice, stroked a finger down the fatty scales. The fish was so large it felt boneless, swollen with good food and saltwater. Its gray mouth was set grimly, as though still holding a hook.

"The only thing fresher is what's swimming in the bay." He lowered the lid, his arm brushing her skin, and she pulled her hand back as though scorched. "There's more in the house."

"You said you'll take a check?" she asked, turning to look up at him. He grinned. "What's so funny?"

"You," he said. "Come in the house. We'll talk business. You drink?"

"Coffee," she said.

He shrugged, touched her shoulder. "You're the boss."

†

She filled out Sam and Kate's check for three thousand dollars, made out to *Simon Tyee Black, Coos Bay Chinook*. He looked over her shoulder while she held the pen, spelling his name when she hesitated. "I thought it was a nickname."

"It is," he said, and from her, put the check under the flour canister on the counter. The kitchen was grandmotherly, all yellow crockery and matching blue pots, but dingy, as though whatever old lady had owned the pieces never got around to using them. A dented copper kettle sat on the table, a tiny web in the crotch of the spout. A prism hung over the sink, and a macrame owl stared down at the unmade futon in the corner. One room, with a table and a chair, a two-burner stove, and a third freezer covered in lures and ties. A shaggy dog that whined from the bed until Simon put it outside. The ceiling, unpainted dark wood, seemed low, and Betsy found herself whispering as though in a church.

"How long have you lived here?" she asked. The flat blade of an oar hung over the bed, curved as an eye. The smell of dog food, brackish water.

"I'm passing through. Just a few seasons, then I go back North." He got the coffee from the cabinet, filled the dusty kettle and set it on the stove.

She put her hands on her hips, wishing that her dress had pockets.

He smiled over his shoulder, and she blushed. She hadn't been alone with a man since her marriage—there was no computer here, no artificial lights even. A gull called from the cove, a high screel that sounded like an ambulance siren. She shivered, thinking of how quiet it was here, how far away the other houses. There was nobody to tell her she was doing the wrong thing.

"You'll help me load the coolers?" she asked Simon.

He poured hot water into the coffee filter, lifted the cone to check that the liquid flowed through. "Be patient, boss. One thing at a time." He pointed to the chair, and she lowered herself into it, resting her palms on the table. A few grains of sand had worked themselves into the grooves of the wood, and she picked at them thoughtlessly, the mica shimmering under her fingernails. He put a cup of coffee in front of her, black.

"Thank you," she said. He didn't move away. His fingers touched her hair, the backs of her ears. He traced the tendons on the back of her neck, the fine down on her nape. Then, his voice against her ear.

"Tell your man I drove a hard bargain."

She held her breath. The steam from the coffee filled her nose, a dark, rank smell. She didn't drink it black, could she tell him that?

He kissed her ear, and his hand felt lower down, touching her collarbone and then her breast. He whispered, "Let's not hurry."

She closed her eyes, leaned back in the chair. The single room evaporated—the whole world was his lips on her skin, her awareness shrinking to a single delicious point. He skinned off her clothes and his own, showing the animals that crept and swam and flew under the cloth. And when his body dug into hers, she laughed at the simplicity of it, the strangeness and the ease—didn't everyone do this? All the time? It was as though, after years of waiting, someone had finally connected the broken circuit in her head, and her body was zipping with energy, her nerves firing like platinum pistons.

‡

"Did you bring the eggs?" Dave asked. "I finally found some wi-fi. The neighbors must have turned on their router."

She found a pat of butter in the fridge, sniffed it. "I got the fish," she said, putting a frying pan on the stove. "Good bargain, too. Three thousand for everything he had ready."

Dave looked up from his computer screen, smiled. "Honey, you don't know the first thing about negotiation."

The butter foamed, and she turned the heat to low before it browned. She picked up the first egg and held it over the pan. "I did alright."

He shook his head. She heard the swish of a scimitar, canned howling. Then, a few minutes later, a moan.

"At least I got what I came for," she said. The egg cracked neatly between her thumbs, and its yolk swam in the hot butter like a salmon that, having spawned, goes in circles, waiting to die.

II

THE BEREAVED

In February, Angela found herself at the edge of the duck pond at Laurelhurst Park. The cold water was murky with breadcrumbs. A few bald mallards and Canada geese circled nearby, hopeful. Angela watched them until her vision blurred, then eased herself onto a bench under a fading blue and yellow pavilion, its concrete foundation dotted with swallow droppings. She closed her eyes, studied the red clouds on the insides of her lids. Her shoes, wet from the grass, flopped open in a V.

A jogger passed behind her, shoes loud on the gravel. Her cell phone rang once, and she turned it off without looking at the lit screen. She knew it was Danny, who'd call over and over, leaving at least one pissed off message and one apologetic message and maybe even one worried message. *Where are you? Can we meet up? I'm sorry.* She palmed the phone in her raincoat pocket, let her thumb tickle the buttons, but didn't turn it back on. *Let him suffer,* she thought. *Let him call and get mad and figure out whose fault this really is.*

It was beginning to drizzle again. The sky did not change, a cloudy ceiling shedding a gray glare that dulled the leaves, the birds, the worn toes of Angela's sneakers—the things that had shone that summer, when she'd been newly in love, sober for once, ready to start over. Now, Angela watched the wood table by the pond slowly absorb the spitting rain. The water drummed like fingertips, slowly peeling the weak paint from the wood.

"Excuse me," said a voice. His hand was on the bench, and Angela's eyes swam up his wiry arm to his wide-set blue eyes. He had a mole hidden in one eyebrow, and it pulled his face into a disbelieving look.

"Do you have a light?"

She handed him her matches, smiled when he fumbled the tiny box. He looked familiar—the way all men looked familiar these days, interchangeable under dim tavern lights. "Trade you for a cigarette," she said.

The smoke rose in weak columns, collecting in the struts of the roof.

"Nice accent. Atlanta?"

"New Orleans."

"Huh," he said, handing the matches back. "You're a long way from home."

"Portland is home," she said, trying to keep the slur out of her voice. She'd downed two Bloody Marys back at the diner, and they were hooking into her tongue, elongating her vowels and making her second-guess herself. "Do I know you?"

He sat at the opposite end of the bench, stretching his legs out as though warming them at an invisible fire. "Probably not."

She leaned her chin on her fist. "I've seen you somewhere."

"Maybe. I'm Roy." He extended his hand, cigarette stuck in the corner of his mouth. They shook, solemnly.

The gravel, dark gray, was turning to puddles, and the fractured pavilion window was dotted with water. A homeless man, wrapped in a soggy sleeping bag, staggered past. No shopping cart, not even a hand out for change. His hair, filthy and dreadlocked, protruded like angry thoughts from his head.

The phone twanged again, a single bright tone. She ignored it, crossed her arms.

That morning she couldn't find the toy-machine ring that Danny had given her, the one that left a graphite whisper on her finger. Not even a real diamond, and she'd had to put the coin in the machine herself. Insisting to her parents *we're engaged, we're engaged*, though he hadn't proposed, even when she begged. And then waking up to find the ring was gone, as though Danny had somehow slipped it off her finger, thrown it away as easily as a penny. That's what started it. No ring. She wouldn't listen to his reasons for wanting to wait, as he put it. Another excuse to delay—when he knew how badly she needed to be loved, to prop herself up on somebody who cared. She drank too quickly while they argued. As usual. And he pretended nothing was wrong, even when she raised her voice and the other customers turned to look at them, the loud girl and her boyfriend who mopped his plate with a bite of pancake over and over, as though writing secret letters in the syrup. Their words were briars, just waiting for the opportunity to catch one another's clothes.

She chewed the cigarette, then ground the filter under her heel. She hadn't been hungover this morning, which seemed a good enough reason to keep drinking the way she had the night before. Danny had raised his eyebrows when she ordered the second Bloody Mary. And then he'd taken the car keys from her. She called him a motherfucker and kicked the driver's side door so hard it left a dent. She'd kicked Danny, too. He didn't dent but he bruised and swore. Faces in the diner window, watching them. *You are such a crazy bitch, Angela*, he hissed. How many messages had he left, she wondered.

"You waiting on somebody?" Roy asked.

"Just sitting." She glanced at him. "Like you."

"Hope you don't mind the company," he said.

She smiled, trying to look winning and cheeky. "Don't mind, don't matter."

He turned away, expressionless. He wore black boots, the toes long and curved like hooves. A tattoo curled on his wrist, illegible—she blinked, trying to read the coiled letters, but he put his hands in his coat.

The ducks, discouraged by the rain, clustered on the small mound in the middle of the pond, finding shelter under the crippled willow tree and sprawling azaleas. Angela watched them settle into the mud, the females disappearing against the earth. The geese folded their long necks across their backs.

"You drink whiskey?" Roy asked. The flask's mouth opened towards her. She eyed the shiny stopper, Roy's clean fingernails, and coat cuff. "Good day for it."

She glanced around, then took it from his hand. The taste stung her eyes, made her nostrils close in a gasp. "That's good."

"Help yourself."

She took three sips, keeping her eyes on the immovable clouds as she tipped her head back. After this, she might go to a bar. That meant she couldn't have any more than six sips of whiskey, maybe seven. Those, in combination with her double Bloody Mary from breakfast, might make her slur or stumble, which meant she wouldn't be able to buy anything stronger than iced tea anywhere else. It might be cheaper to just pick up a fifth of something at the liquor store near her apartment, hole up with a movie, and pass out. Get up in time for work tomorrow. But, she thought, scanning the well-dressed stranger, it might be easier to find trouble exactly where she was. Anyway, Danny was likely to be waiting for her, sitting on the stoop of her building, ready to yell the moment she appeared. She didn't look forward to that, knew she couldn't take the criticism without more anesthetic. There were men everywhere she went, and they had money. And she needed something extra today, just to get her over the hump and sliding down into the February evening.

"Thank you," she said, handing back the flask. Her elbows cushioned by the smooth armrest, the bones in her legs turning to liquid gold as the whiskey seeped through her.

"Sure," Roy nodded, glancing at her. "Those ducks are going at it again." There was a squabble, a flapping. One tumbled into the water.

"You come here a lot?" she asked. Watched him nurse the flask against the buttons of his shirt. The tattoo appearing, then receding under his cuff.

"Since November," he said. "Usually there's no pretty girl to sit with, though."

"Thank you," she said, knowing that she was repeating herself as the words bumbled off her tongue. *Pretty girl*. She meant to ask if he always sat here, just as she meant to ask if he was done with the crossword puzzle so meticulously folded and peeking from his pocket with a ballpoint tucked beside it. She intended, whiskey at hand, to sit nearer to him and finish the crossword in a way that he would find charming, in a way that would entice him to take her home with or without knowing her name or anything about her, and she intended fervently in that moment as she saw his fine long-boned hands sliding over the stainless steel flask and his blue-fierce eyes and the scruff that only a hungover and single man's jaw can grow and the way his hips pressed into the wood on his side of the bench she wished to go home with him and lie on his pale-green sheets and watch the muffled shapes move across his ceiling and sleep with the taste of someone new in her mouth.

He drank again, nodded to the ducks. "Human company. You know."

"Well, I'm not a regular," she said, laughed too loudly at her own joke.

His mouth twitched, flattened. "November," he said.

She touched her eyebrow, absentmindedly, the place where his mole burrowed into the dark hairs.

He said, "I used to bring flowers, but people would steal them. Kids. The ducks tore them up. So now it's just the whiskey. You don't mind, do you?"

She didn't.

He shifted his pointed boots again, crossing his ankles one way and another. She wished for another drink, but he cradled the flask to his chest and did not offer it. He kept his eyes on the pond, the rings spreading in the shallows, the ground filthy with seeds. His damp hair curled over his ears in dark flames, and she stared at him until her eyes watered. The cigarette smoke lingered in her nose, mixing with the brackish smell of the water, disintegrating mold.

"You didn't hear about it, did you?" he asked. Her head snapped up—had she been dozing?

She rubbed her mouth, tried to catch up.

"There were fliers everywhere. And it was on the news. Tragedy, tragedy." He squinted into the flask.

"Sorry." She wanted to look interested, sympathetic. If the whiskey was not forthcoming, maybe he'd offer another cigarette.

"She drowned here," he said. "Some family found her when they went to feed the ducks. Already half rotted." He swigged. "I had to identify the body. Face gone, teeth showing through the skin. I shouldn't have said that. Forget I said that."

"Who?" Angela felt a surge of nausea. She bit her lip.

"Michelle, Ma Belle," he sang, light and out of key. "My girlfriend. You didn't see her on the news?"

"Was there a—trial?"

"Suicide. She quit taking her meds, disappeared for a few days." He pointed at the ducks. "They're probably the only witnesses."

She tried to focus, keeping her gaze on the folded crossword. The blue ink crawled across the paper, illegible. "Your girlfriend?"

"I visit almost every day," he said. "She'd hate that."

She watched him tap out another cigarette, roll it between his fingers so that the tobacco crackled in the paper. He touched the corner of his eye, shook his head.

"She hated me."

A couple passed, sharing an oversized umbrella. Angela could hear their voices as though underwater, the vowels distorted.

"She was the one," Roy said. He twiddled the stopper, this way and that. His eyes locked onto Angela's, so blue that she could barely breathe. "Why are you looking at me like that?"

Her head wobbled. Her phone vibrated in her pocket, and she clutched it, her hands shaking against its battery. "You loved her."

"We drove each other crazy." He lifted the flask to his lips, his jaw long and handsome. She watched him gray at the edges, her vision popping with stars.

She could understand what he *meant*, but the words skated over her slippery skull. She could have kissed him, could have tried to ease her pain against his. But he wouldn't give her the flask. His eyebrows drew together over his forehead, making the mole disappear with a look that said, *You don't want to know how horrible we were.* So she slapped her shoes down, hard enough to make her feet tingle. Make herself want to get away. It was hard to balance, her legs changing length on the uneven ground. As she walked away, she had the idea that he would be impressed with her and the way she could hold her liquor, the way she chose to apologize so kindly to him and offer her condolences. Maybe the glaring clouds would illuminate her paper-thin dress and cast strange shadows on her hair as she left, and he would run after her down the street and beg to take her home where there was a bottle of Champagne in the refrigerator and a cat that would bump her with its tabby-scruff chin. She shouldered her purse and although she paused in the arch of the pavilion, ready to be admired, he did not try to stop her and when she turned on her cell phone she had six voicemails and they were all from Danny and her stomach, already brimming with alcohol and several bites of old breakfast, felt like a pit of lead.

"Hello?" she asked casually, holding the phone slightly away from her head. She stopped under the eaves of a brick building that used to be a bathhouse and was now a place where little girls learn to dance. She meant to sound pleasantly surprised.

"Where are you?" he asked. "I've been calling for two hours straight. Why didn't you answer your phone?"

"Didn't realize it was off," she said. The rain spattered her face and she pressed her spine against the rough wall. Her tongue scraped her teeth, and even she could smell the booze, thick and rank as a lie. "I'm downtown."

"You're slurring."

Her dress was getting damp, the flowers darkening on the fabric and sticking to her skin.

"You should go home. Get a cab."

There was a long silence, then she heard the sparkwheel of his lighter and his breath, the smoke, crisp against the receiver. She slid down and sat on the sidewalk, politely tucking her feet in so that anyone could walk by. She wouldn't be in the way. It was important to think of these things—they said a lot about a person.

She missed the South, in a wash of feelings that spread through her lungs like molasses. She missed the diners with ashtrays on the tables, bottomless cups of coffee. She missed the boys who wore their baseball hats backwards, held the door and offered a dip of their Skoal tobacco still warm from their backpockets. She missed living in a place where a good man might be hard to find, but not hard to keep once you had him.

"I thought we were going to get married," she said. Her voice sticky. Her fingers soft from the rain, the white hands of a drowned woman.

He sighed again. The rain began in earnest. A taxi went by, its light off. She felt the water running down her hair and into her ears. It would saturate the phone, short out the battery. "Angela," he said, and his voice was so distant, so reasonable, that she started to cry.

"Why not?" she moaned. "Why not?"

III

RUNAWAY

*L*isten. I dreamed that I woke up in a city that was enough like Berlin to trick my dreaming mind into believing I woke up in our old flat, and that you were just in the other room, in the silent moment between two tasks, about to crack an egg over the hot plate or switch on the coffee grinder; in the dream, it was important that you were close by, because I felt safe and loved, in the warm white sheets that still carried the scent and softness of our sleeping bodies. The sky was the color of an American nickel and, because it was a dream, time didn't matter to me. I was just happy to be there.

The best part was the slow realization of where I was coming over me— peeling back the sheet tented over my head, recognizing the black iron nightstand with your military flashlight on it and my red-covered book. I saw one more time the room's undecorated high, barely lilac walls; the crack in the corner that was stained the color of saffron; the letter from my mother open on the little desk by the full French windows that went from ceiling to floor and showed me a partial view of Old Berlin, with its rooftops and chimney covers painted in a faintly golden wash I have since come to associate only with memory, or fairy tales, and those particularly magic weeks I spent alone with you between jobs, when we were so generous with our love.

In the dream, I picked up the letter and although it was written in hieroglyphics my sleeping brain made sense of it and the snakey letters resolved into a page of numbers, my name at the top like a cashier's receipt. I ran my finger down its columns. Even in my dreams, I was impenitent. In the next room, I heard a record playing. The sound faded as I receded from sleep, until it was only the soprano of a passing police siren.

I was not in Berlin anymore, or strung out, and I missed both of those things, and you, with an ache that pulled on me like gravity, holding me fast to this sweet, secret planet we created together. I've forgotten what your voice sounds like, but I've held on to every word you said to me.

The first time we shared a needle, you looked into my eyes as you pushed the dope into my vein. "Your eyes are doves," you said, and I felt myself melting into you. Our blood mingled in the murky syringe. You always did me first, turning away from me to set up the spoon and the cotton, so I couldn't see how. You cleaned the works, you called the dealer. You handled the cash that I earned, set up my dates. You protected me. This was part of our love.

I can never donate blood, because of you.

After my sentencing I was too weak to leave my cot. They searched my room every day while I lay there. The counselors checked my arms for tracks, took the sheets off, and even searched the cavities of my body with their rubber fingers. There was nothing to find.

I remembered too many things; our last days together were fresh in my mind and they pricked me when I drifted close. The scene at customs, when they separated us. You used to say that you could feel it when I was thinking about you. Was that ever true? Or did you say it because you knew I thought about you all the time, so there was never a minute when you weren't in my mind? I read your palm once, playing around, and saw my own face in it. Do you remember that?

I slept, but my heart was awake. My dreams were too real. I wrote down nothing, even though my counselor gave me a notepad and my own pack of new, bright markers. She was old, sober. The hatchet mark between her eyebrows deepened as she went through the answers on my intake forms.

"I was in a bad place," I said.

"It sounds like it. What were you doing in—"

"Just traveling. Like, as a student."

She looked at me closely. I widened my eyes, which always made me look younger.

"When was the last time you ate?"

"I don't really do that."

One of the aides brought me cocoa and a pack of neon orange crackers. My counselor turned to the next page, scanned it, and looked at me again. Eyes to the paper. Eyes to my face. Back and forth.

She had done bad things, but she wasn't a criminal. Like me.

"Why do you feel you'd benefit from inpatient?"

"I don't want to die," I said.

She nodded, made a note. Everything I said after that was a lie. But they let me in, and like you told me, that was the most important part of any story: the part where they start to believe you.

The morning after I dreamed about Berlin, I woke up in my real bed, in my actual life, and took a long look out the window. It was good being in a place without bars on the windows. In my morning group, the topic was gratitude, so I said that, about the bars, and everyone nodded. I didn't mention the violet haze that crowded the edges of my vision, coloring everything lavender, the way I used to see things when I was with you, crossing yet another border to deliver yet another package. I didn't talk in group much, so they treated each word like a miracle, a ruby. They had no idea who I really am.

After morning group, there was a mandatory class about triggers and then a group processing session, and then lunch. I picked at the soggy white biscuit, covered in gravy. The sauce had nubs of sausage and gristle in it, and the longer I looked at it the less I wanted to eat it. All the other girls complained about getting fat while they doubled up on slabs of thickly frosted chocolate cake. I slid my tray to the girl on my right and she made my meal disappear. Chocolate has caffeine in it. I watched her eat. Chocolate is different from methamphetamines.

There was the usual chatter. Negative self-talk, things we had done or narrowly missed doing, the boyfriends we hoped were waiting for us on the outside. I listened, adding nothing. The small black thing inside me crouched, waiting. They thought I was brain dead. They called me Zombie Girl.

"We get passes today," Brittany said.

Not everyone got passes. She was just bragging.

Tiff said, "I'm going to get my nails done," and that meant she had money.

"Who's going with you?"

I didn't ask for it, but my name was on the pass list at the front desk. My counselor—she wanted me out more. There were three of us, for accountability. I was supposed to go with Melissa to drop off a resume at H&M and then with Brittany to watch her get a manicure. I saw the impatience on their faces when they saw my name next to theirs. *Great. Zombie Girl.* I didn't bother smiling, just took my slip and went to my room to get my purse. I fingered my latest passport, hidden in its lining. I'd been clean for more than 30 days. My head was clear. I knew how to trade everything. It was time to make my move.

The others were waiting for me downstairs by the security door. Brittany was wearing a bright, bubblegum-pink hoodie with the name of a tourist trap on it; Melissa opted for something low cut and bejeweled. Their hair was styled in matching messy buns with identical pieces pulled out around their temples. Even their sobriety dates were the same. To me, they looked like Rehab Tweedle Dee and Tweedle Dum.

"Is that what you're wearing?" Brittany asked me.

It was a matted, black angora sweater you'd bought for me in Monaco. I cut all the tags out of my clothes, but this one was a Lagerfeld. My whole suitcase was designers, originals. One of the things you said you liked about me was that you could dress me in Chanel and I'd still look like a high-end hooker.

I shrugged. "It's what I have."

They walked 15 feet ahead of me. I could smell their cigarette smoke but couldn't hear their gossip. One of them looked over her shoulder and gave me a mean little half-smile. I couldn't hate them too much. Melissa got raped by her brother with a Louisville Slugger in the family den while her uncle and dad watched, drinking Coors Light. Brittany sucked dick at truck stops in exchange for tweak, rides, and orange soda. Low-grade shit.

They were both way younger than they looked. But I saw them the way you would see them, and I was too smart not to see them for what they were. In group, their fat faces leaked crocodile tears and they said the right recovery-sounding phrases and got the leader nodding and making notes on his clipboard. That was one thing I did have in common with them: we were impossible to trust.

H&M was big and hollow. The other two went inside together, to drop off the application, and I stood around out front with my hands in my pockets. I was good at waiting. Sometimes the door opened and I caught a phrase of electronic music. It reminded me of the club where I met you, in Hackesche Höfe, right before things started to get interesting for me. That night, I was out by myself, because I'd managed to fight with all my friends and nobody wanted to dance with me. It was about to be my birthday but I didn't care, I was so lonely and miserable. Bored. I had a few shots of chilled vodka at the bar and was turning around to get a look at the DJ when you elbowed me and said that if I didn't smile you were going to tell me to sulk somewhere else. You were tall, lanky under your leather jacket, and had a hand rolled cigarette behind your ear.

"Are you the Thought Police?" I asked.

"Bouncer," you said. "I'm joking. I'm playing the next set. And I don't want to look out here and see any pretty girls pouting."

"How did you know I was an American?"

You smirked. "You just told me."

It was the easiest thing, to leave with you at the end of the night. And stay the whole week in your bed, smoking hash in your flat, getting up to drink milk straight from the carton and then lying down with you again.

"You're like a baby," you said.

"So innocent," you smiled. "All you want is milk and sleep. You even smell like a baby."

A seventeen-year gap in our ages. Not that we talked about it. I didn't ask about who the girl was before me. I just did what you showed me. I took to the life quickly, easily, and I loved your look of gratification when you saw what I was really capable of.

"When I get out of here, I'm going back to Phoenix," Brittany said. "You can get a mani-pedi for like 14 dollars."

"Portland's too expensive," Melissa echoed.

"I'm not tipping, either," Brittany said. "But I love treating my girl!"

Melissa squealed and pushed her nose into Brittany's neck. That's how it was, in rehab. There was always something changing hands.

I bummed a cigarette as we walked up to the nail salon. The prices were stuck on the wall with white adhesive letters. Half the words were misspelled. $16 NIAL PLUS DIP, they both picked that one.

"You gotta smoke outside," Melissa told me. "And stay close, we have to do what the pass says."

The pass said, stay together no matter what. Don't be back late. Don't do anything that violates the center's code of conduct or interferes with our treatment plans. Girls who broke the rules didn't get second chances—they ended up in jail, serving the rest of their sentences, or else back out on the street trying the game one more time. Those rules did not apply to someone like me.

"How long do we have left?" I asked.

Melissa shrugged. "Back by 4. It's only like 2:30 now. We're gonna say that we went to an AA meeting or something."

I had an hour and a half. Plenty of time.

I watched through the plate glass while they settled their fat asses into the massage chairs, put their feet into the bubbling water, and smiled at one another. In no time, they were leafing through magazines. They forgot about me, and I felt their attention turning to things more immediate: the shade of polish on their toes, the texture of the nail file. It was the right moment to slip away, so I did, the way you taught me, vaporizing like a ghost. I flicked the smoke into the gutter, next to the tire of a Lexus, then bent down to look into the car's open window.

The driver stared at me, startled. One hand on the wheel, the other on his phone.

"You look bored," I said. "Can I get in?"

This was how it always went, when it went my way. He nodded. By the time I was settled into the passenger's seat, his hand was on my knee.

"Where can I take you?" he asked.

I laughed, the way men liked, and checked my reflection in the mirror on the back of the sun visor. Sober or not, I was still a 10. It was reassuring that, no matter where I went, the men and I were still the same.

"Let's do it fast," I said. I put my hand on the gear shift. "I don't have to be anywhere, do you?"

Twenty minutes later I had a mouth full of his cum and $200 in twenties tucked into the crotch of my panties. He kept his hand on the back of my neck the whole time. I did the trick you taught me, love.

"You're sweet," I said.

"I've never done this before."

"Me neither," I lied.

This game was always too easy. When I worked him over like I did it wasn't because I liked it; I had to have the money, and my need sharpened my hustle. When they caught us in the Frankfurt airport, we were detained separately—you would have been turned back to Berlin, most likely, for the key of heroin they found concealed in your luggage. I was arrested as an accessory, sent to treatment on a pity plea. I didn't struggle. It was just time apart, and I knew that no matter where you were, I would find you. I had my passport, and the only weapon I needed was the body that I lived in. I swallowed and wiped my mascara from under my eyes.

"You have to go?"

"Shouldn't I?" Maybe my solution was closer than I thought. *Thank God for porn*, I thought. It made every sex thing believable, for them. It transformed me from a risk into wish fulfillment.

He hesitated. "What if I want more?"

"Drive me somewhere," I said.

The rest was so easy, baby. I picked up right where I'd stopped, and I was just as good as I'd ever been. By the end of the hour, we were checked into the Benson and I had my legs up in the air and he was sweet-talking me on all the things he was going to do for me once he was done fucking the living Christ out of my hot, baby-tight little pussy. I didn't have to wait long. He talked himself into cumming too fast, this time on my belly, and I rolled away before he could collapse on me.

His wallet was on the desk. Are you surprised that I slid so quickly in this direction? Were you tricked by my dream, my soft memories of Berlin? Did you forget that, underneath my sickness, I was a beautiful monster, a creature created without a conscience?

The man put his arm over his eyes. "Wow," he said, the way men do after sex. They can never find anything profound to say—not like you, who talked poetry to me all the time.

The wallet had five credit cards in it and more cash. He was holding out on us. The keys, too, I took. And his phone. I heard the first soft snore and slipped back into my clothes.

"My boyfriend's napping," I said to the front desk attendant. "If he calls down, please tell him I'm picking up his shirts."

One trick after another, and they all fucking worked. I went down to the valet and got the Lexus—only a quarter tank of gas, but I wasn't going that far. I thought of the two girls in the nail salon, who by now would be standing out on the sidewalk with those foam things between their toes, gawping up and down the street looking for me, paper passes turning to mush in their sweaty hands, increasingly anxious to find me before curfew, waddling back to treatment while smoking and cussing me and rehearsing their story until it was completely airtight and consistent, why was I gone, where did Kayla the Zombie Girl go. I found a pack of Newports in the glove box and lit one. The mint oil stuck with me all the way to the airport.

The next part was so easy, baby, it went like clockwork. Parked in short-term and pulled my hair and makeup together, so I looked less like a runaway and more like an art student. I bought a one-way ticket with my ride's credit cards using the app on his phone. Used his frequent flier miles to upgrade myself to first class. Downloaded the boarding pass. Put on his sunglasses and took a simple black gym bag from his trunk so I'd have luggage to carry. There was no chance I could use the credit cards again—

he'd be waking up by now, conscious and panicked—so I left them in the console. I had his cash and my imitation passport, and that was all I needed.

The greatest high in the world isn't something you can buy. I wish I'd said that to the group, when I was in rehab. Holding myself apart like that—I was sober, but that was all. The more days I put between myself and my last fix, the stronger my confidence in myself got. I knew I could go like a hot knife through butter, without a habit to slow me down. The other girls sold themselves and stole shit for the sole purpose of feeding their cravings. Me—I did it because I was good at it, and you loved that about me, when we were together. In the bar that night, you lifted my hair away from my shoulder and smiled and said the prettiest thing about me was that I didn't have any morals. We were made for each other.

I was sweating under my Lagerfeld by the time I got into the terminal. A thin exhilarating sheen of wet coated my armpits and the spot between my shoulder blades. Better than drugs, and my skin was zinging with adrenaline. I scanned the boarding pass at security and handed over the passport.

"One way?" the TSA agent asked.

"Back for the summer term," I said, smiled my American Girl smile. I wasn't a zombie anymore. I was awake now, the active darkness inside me writhed with happiness, something to do other than be good all the time.

The flight I'd managed to book departed in less than an hour, a pricey Lufthansa overnight to Amsterdam. I had nothing metal except the Lexus keys, which I dropped into the needle exchange box in the women's bathroom. Then, I walked slowly towards the gate, loving the way my knees shook. I made myself pause to look in the gift shop windows, stop to leaf through a magazine before putting it back on the rack. I saw nothing but sensed everything.

They weren't going to find me. That was the best feeling of all. In treatment I learned that if you're already fucked up, everything is a trigger. I felt that now, sitting at the window by the gate's welcome desk. Every breath heightened my awareness, and I was glad for the sunglasses, because my pupils must have been enormous. I watched the businessmen arrive with their briefcases, European women pulling rolling luggage, none of them giving me a second glance. I was invisible among them and I watched from behind the dark lenses, measuring them, mentally rifling through their belongings.

How far do you think I can go? They won't find me here—there might be a police cruiser in Chinatown with my name on their list of people to look out for. But not the airport. Not in first class. Not my window seat with the reclining headrest and the flute of Brut Rosé that I accept with the clumsy charm of a girl who might have been treated to this flight by her father, who loves her, who is wealthy and far away, and wishes her every comfort and amusement while she's suspended in midair for hours and hours like a princess in a coffin that flies to you, love, over a blackened sea and carrying a pearl in her belly that she can't help but swallow again and again and again.

I'll be there tomorrow, love.

I can't wait to start where we left off.

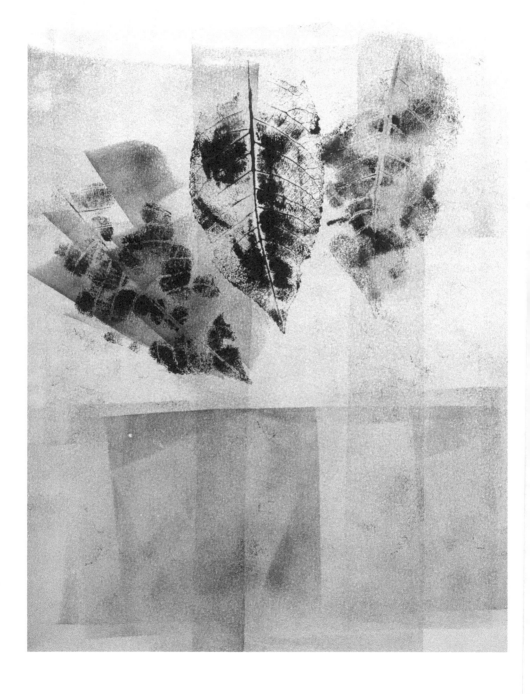

IV

FIDELITY

I waited a year after my husband's suicide to start dating again. Theodor was never far from my mind, of course—a decade with one man will do that—but I didn't want to explain my sudden reemergence into single life. Anyone who was bold enough to ask, I told them I had just gotten out of something serious and was trying to find myself again. Or I lied and said he couldn't keep up with me sexually, something cheap to put off further questioning.

I knew I didn't come off as a vamp, so this was a good answer for me to give. It created confusion. I was not at all interested in being pinned down. Theodor knew me, and now he was dead. I wasn't yet ready to lay the burden of myself on someone new.

I put my photo and a few sentences online, on one of the newer dating apps, and got a flurry of responses. I said yes to everyone, even the lewd ones who said I looked like I give great head (I don't, and I don't). I went on dates with all kinds. There were bankers and lawyers, perverts and plumbers. There was a cartoonist who took me to see a Godard movie; he embarrassed me with his exclamations. One man, in a severe gray suit, said nothing for the duration of the date; as I reached the bottom of my Singapore Sling, he pushed an index card to me across the table. In meticulous block letters it said, "May I eat your ass tonight, you filthy slut?" I smiled, took my purse, and went home to sit in the closet with Theodor's clothes. They smelled like him. He had known my appetites in our marriage, and it wasn't difficult to summon a vision of him, touching me the way he knew I loved. My body missed him. My heart was on the fence.

Things I was not interested in: being a widow, acting out my grief, changing the sheets, taking advice from anyone, journaling, rearranging our place, speaking of him in the past tense, changing my name back from his, getting a cat.

Things I was interested in: continuing as though nothing was wrong, continuing as though instead of dying Theodor was going to reenter life as easily as he'd left it, being alone without being lonely, being lonely as a substitute for grieving, work, running, and going on dates.

I was skinny then, because I ran so much. It was a noticeable change. The first year of our marriage we went to a family reunion; I'd gained back the twenty pounds I lost for the wedding, plus a few more. I was happy and into a routine of baking on the weekends. Theodor's sister looked me up and down and curled her lacquered lip: "Good thing you're already married," she said.

Now I was skinnier than she ever was and I ran 80 kilometers a week: ten every day, and a longer route on Saturdays. When the dating app asked me about my body type, I put 'athletic.'

"You are in good shape," the tailor said when we met. "But not muscular."

He circled my upper arm with his finger and thumb.

"It's temporary," I said.

He shrugged. "Bodies change. This is my business."

At work, my body didn't matter. I'd started at the company shortly after Theodor died: a welcome distraction. I edited technical writing, manuals and handbooks for programmers and electricians. I felt like a brain in a bubble half the time, annotating the errors in red digital ink. It was good, consistent work that paid well, but at the end of the day I was more than ready for my ten kilometers. When I ran, I felt like I was pounding the sadness out of myself, or at least my thoughts of my sadness.

"How long does it take you to sew on a button?" I asked.

"Are you serious?"

His eyebrows drew together. I noticed, for the first time, the austere cut of his suit and the fine, soft cotton shirt he wore, without a tie. The buttons on that shirt were the palest blue, the color of the sky at the end of a night out dancing. I realized that he had probably made this suit and shirt himself, and I was sorry I had asked such an idiotic question.

"I'm trying to make conversation," I said.

"Would you like to see my hands and fingers, as well?" he asked. "Check me for pinpricks?"

"This is not a fairy tale," I said.

"So, yes. It is not necessary."

In Prague at that time, there were tailors on every corner. Some ran dry cleaning businesses or consignments for tailor-made secondhand clothes. Simple fixes like buttons and zippers, or letting down a hem— this was common work. The tailor, Johann, was not Czech and did not make simple repairs. He was in demand, he said, with the stage people. He originally came to Prague with a Berlin ballet troupe, found that there was plenty of work in the city, and decided to stay. I guessed, but wasn't certain, that there was a woman in his story somewhere. I was frightened to ask him. He was by turns ferocious and attentive, and as reluctant as I was to share anything about himself. Now, instead of tutus and tulle, he sewed costumes and gowns for competitive beauty and sport contests. Skimpy, strappy dresses for pageants; glittering skating uniforms, carefully stitched according to the sport's regulations; leotards covered in applique and sequins. He could take a woman and make her look like a goddess, he said, and word of mouth brought him more business than he could handle.

"My assistant sews the buttons," he said, with a wry smile.

Then I knew that he liked me.

He took me to his favorite cafe, near Zlata Ulichka. We sat for an hour drinking Italian-style espressos and watching groups of tourists pass by, like brightly colored clouds. Johann had a sharp eye and made me laugh several times with his observations. I liked immediately the way he saw things. He had a way of bringing a tiny detail into focus, which changed the entire meaning of everything else in the frame.

He spotted, for example, a woman's untied shoe, which caused her to kneel spontaneously near the fountain. "Praying to the Infant of Prague?" A group of Japanese, all armed with selfie sticks, he found noteworthy as well. "Make a collection of their pictures, you'll see a collage of their duck faces, with a tiny bit of city in the background," he said. "I loathe camera phones. They turn the world into a backdrop, when in reality we are just a droplet of sound and movement dancing on its surface."

I asked him about the ballet troupe, and he countered with questions about my job. I made it sound as boring as possible, since first of all I knew it was dull and also because I wanted him to be attracted to me, and I knew that it would take more than technical manuals to hold the interest of a man as clever as he.

"What made you stay in Prague?" I asked. "The truth, really."

"I like that nobody pays for the trolleys," he said.

"Berlin is different?"

"Another world," he said. "And besides, the women are beautiful here. Beautifully dressed."

I was glad I'd worn my good red blouse, instead of something kitschy and Soviet. It had been a long time since a man had looked at me closely— that is not discrediting my husband, marriage would make anyone's gaze less sharp, and in any case he was quite out of sorts at the end of his life. I realized that the men who clicked on my picture on the dating app were responding perhaps to a recognizable collection of desirable features, and not really taking time to *see* me, measure me, the way that Johann was at this very moment. "We make our own clothes," I said. "This, I made."

"I can see that," he said.

I bit my lip. It probably looked like a scarlet sack to him. I wondered if the seams were puckered.

"My business is making clothes that women cannot make for themselves. In Germany, I worked also for performers with unusual bodies. You know."

"Ballerinas?"

"Them, yes, but also the burlesques."

"We don't have that kind of nightclub in Prague."

"Yes, you do. You simply don't know—your kind of person doesn't go places like that."

I could feel myself turning the same shade as my blouse. Suddenly, I was ready to leave. I fastened the clasp on my purse and gave my date a businesslike smile.

"Perhaps we are too different," I said. "I am glad that we at least share a taste for good coffee."

"Please don't go," he said. He put his hand on my wrist. "I've insulted you."

"I don't like assumptions being made," I said. "It sounds to me like your glamorous life has spoiled you for anyone who is not flashy. I am no cabaret dancer."

His pressure on my wrist increased, almost imperceptibly. A very thin young woman, clutching a volume of Kafka, stalked by, staring down at a paper map. "I'm sorry," Johann said. "This is not my stage. I have acted badly."

I shrugged, letting myself play the part of the pouting girlfriend. It had been a long time since I'd been in that role. I remembered what I'd been like at 20, so beautiful. In my mind, that period was a series of short film clips, which all concluded in me tossing my hair and walking away from a boy who dared to say the wrong thing. Now, I wore a braid, and I had learned to merely take in men's stupid observations, keeping still while their words grazed the surface of my skin. Sometimes, I imagined holding their sentences up on the electric screen of my mind so that I could render each phrase into bloody fragments. But always, I was calm, my face smooth. I looked at Johann with my placid face on.

"Did they think you were a queer in Berlin?" I asked, and was gratified when he scowled. "Here, you can be artistic. But men who sew might have a different reputation in Western Europe."

"You don't like criticism."

"I don't like criticism that is founded in opinion and not fact."

"Then you'll find plenty to be offended by."

We were quiet for a moment. I still had my bag on my lap; his hand had not moved away from my wrist.

He cleared his throat. "An old lady is watching us," he said. "She looks scandalized; do you know her?"

I turned, casually, and glanced over my shoulder, as though a sound or sudden movement had caught my passing attention. The woman, in a quilted lavender coat, sat on a bench near the holy fountain. Her shopping bags were beside her, taking up just enough space that she didn't have to share her seat. She was holding a crepe sandwich wrapped in paper. It was my landlady. She was eating the crepe slowly.

"She's probably KGB," I said, trying to make light of it. I moved my hand away.

"In that coat?"

She had a trace of banana cream on her cheek, giving her the air of a naughty child. Her name was Magda, and she manned the office in our building's lobby. It was she who found Theodor's body and called me, breathless, on the telephone. I could hear her wheezing in my ear now.

Where are you? You must come now.

I'm away.

You must. The ambulance is taking him.

I can't, Magda.

You are the wife. You must make an arrangement.

I'd paid her a thousand Euros for her trouble, and hired a cleaning service for the mess of blood and burnt spoons Theodor made in our apartment. She watched me stagger in and out of the lobby at my usual times, wearing work clothes or sweaty from my run. She never commented at the lack of change in my routine, but her look cut through me like an angel's sword. She probably thought I'd killed him—or that I had wished for him to die. It wasn't difficult to imagine her standing over Theodor's body, plucking the folded paper from his chest, reading the scribbled note, and carefully replacing it with a disapproving shake of her head. I had read it too; I knew what he accused me of.

I knew too much about him to pretend that his overdose was an accident.

Although it was a half cloudy day, I took out my sunglasses and put them on. "Let's walk," I said.

"Where would you like to go?"

"Surprise me," I said.

He rose, left a few bills on the table. "I wish to know if I am forgiven."

"I rescind my comments," I said.

As we went to the south end of the street, I could feel Magda's eyes on us. I'd been careful not to bring any of my dates home, in part because I knew she crouched in the office door, her small TV always on, her chair half-turned so she could see the entrance. She, among all the people I saw, was the one who knew I was a widow. In her disapproving face, I saw all that I had failed to become. I had not been a good wife—my husband had died. Now, I failed to mourn him properly. I could not even assume the black mantle of grief, or bother to turn down the corners of my mouth to show my bereaved state. Here I was, wearing the brightest bright red, with lipstick to match, drinking at a foreign cafe with a good-looking man. Magda, within her lavender armor, must have felt each of these failures like a blow.

"That woman is still watching," Johann said.

"She's a dragon. My landlady, and of a certain generation. I'm sure she'd prefer to see me in the chapel, lighting candles at that little doll's feet."

"Praying for a son?"

"We never wanted any."

He nodded. As we came to the end of the street, he turned to glance at the racks of postcards outside one of the tourist shops. There was a pile of tiny Infant of Prague dolls on a table; he picked one up and inspected it. It was wearing a tiny, frilly christening gown. He turned the doll over, frowning.

"How long were you married?" he asked.

"I can't say."

He handled the doll, lifting its petticoat to separate its nude cotton legs, which were just unarticulated fabric tubes with a pinch of sand in the end of each foot. "You didn't like children?"

"Not the way some people do. The light is changing, here."

He put it back and crossed with me, coming to the trolley station by the oblong strip of grass that passed for a city park. Theodor used to joke, *of course it's a park, they've put some turf around the statue who lives there. Hardly any room to stroll, all that nationalism taking up space.* I wished there was less space between Johann and me. We were out of sight of the landlady and making good time—I wondered if he was a runner, too. Or was his body an illusion, the result of good tailoring?

"Some people," he said. "I will tell you something. It was better to let them think I was a queer. Can you imagine? Fondling ballerinas, ten-year-old girls with hard little tits, the wives of wealthy men. I could not have done what I did, had they not believed this about me."

"What did you have to give up?"

"That's a different question."

We crossed through the park and passed under the iron shadow of the statue, a Czech hero in a tailcoat, gesturing towards the center of the city.

"Leni," Johann said. "Why did your husband not want children?"

"I didn't say that. He wanted us to live simply."

"But what you wanted was different?"

"Different, in that it was the same as what everyone wanted. Theodor wanted me all to himself. We were going to be together forever."

"I never married," Johann said. "Divorce is foreign to me."

"There was no divorce. He killed himself last year." I plucked a leaf from a glossy boxwood as we passed it, still gliding steadily towards the St. Charles Bridge. "He left me, after all."

I heard the intake of his breath, but before he could say anything, I shook my head. "Please don't say that you're sorry. I don't want your sympathy."

"That's not it."

We walked further, turning once down a street that was paved in rough cobblestones. I took his arm, so my wedge heels wouldn't be caught on the irregular stones. I liked the feeling of being steadied, of no longer having to carry myself along. The shops were closing their shutters, and a bar clicked on its sign, bulbs popping like a flurry of champagne bubbles.

The bridge at sunset was a popular destination for couples, so Johann and I merely blended into the crowd of men and women. Many of them paused on the sidewalk, heedless of the other sightseers, to press their foreheads together and grin disingenuously at the cameras on their phones. The castle was a low, golden lump on the far bank of the river. The perfect backdrop for the romances unfolding around me. I expected to miss Theodor, or at least feel guilty for enjoying the view with this handsome stranger, but I did not. Once Magda's eyes were off me, I felt no shame at all. I held tightly to Johann's arm. I did not care if I crumpled the fabric. I felt the man underneath the suit and our bodies' contact eased my mind.

He led me to the edge of the bridge so that we could look down. The water was too dark for us to see our reflections.

"I hear him in your voice," he said. "Listen: your words are not yours. You repeat what he told you, without thinking."

"How would you know?"

"After a year, you're not finished with him."

To this, I had no answer.

He continued: "A relationship is truly over only when you stop using the special words and phrases you used to share. Out of heart, out of mouth. When it's over, you cease speaking the same language; your shared codes made love its own private country. Sometimes, this is a deliberate choice, to give up your citizenship and leave your old love's borders. The first few months, when I did this, I was love's refugee. I had no place to go that felt like home. Then, after some time, I was eager to shed my old accent and learn a new language—like any immigrant, eager to disappear into a new city, seamlessly."

I wondered what her name had been.

"In any case," he said, "You must choose. Don't speak one language and dream in another. You'll never be at peace in either place."

"One foot on either bank?" I asked, enjoying the image.

"I came here in difficult circumstances. I can only share my experience. I do not even know if I express myself well in Czech. I feel that I speak in poetry. In German, it is easier, but above all I want to be understood."

I looked down again. "I wish we had a penny to throw in."

"I wish you'd had children."

"I am glad we didn't. He was planning to leave, all along."

"I admire your loyalty," he said. "You speak your language beautifully."

Then his arms were around me, and I felt my grief pouring out like black water, soaking me in something warmer and closer than tears. His tongue entered my mouth and I spread my teeth to receive him, his saliva mixing with mine, our throats humming with stories, names, promises, that we had yet to offer one another.

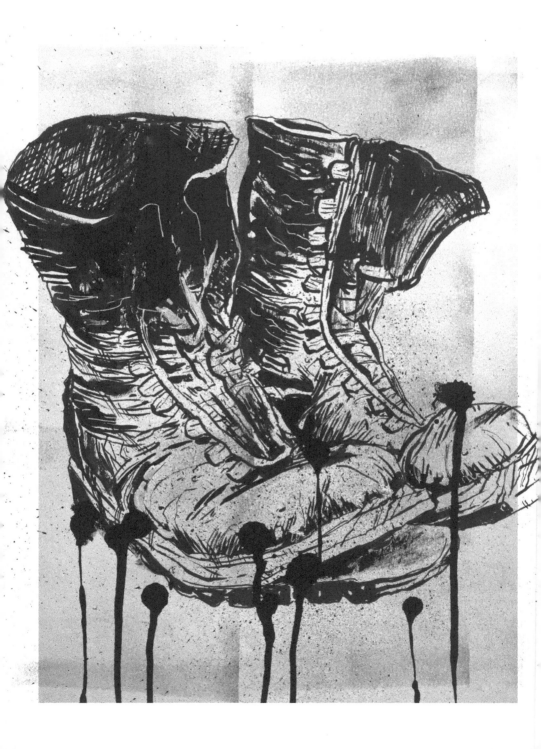

TORCH SONG

Toward the end of work, Barney's hand found the clasp knife in his back pocket and guided it to his cheek. He sheared off a tiny patch of his beard, laid it on the work bench beside the oily clamps, the half-finished iron gate, the mallet with its rubber-wrapped handle. He held a match to the tip of his hairs, watched them blacken and curl like feathers in the flame. He liked the smell, the way the strands didn't crumble to dust but hardened into wires. The match burned down to his fingertips and went out, leaving behind a wisp of sulfur. A white-eyed spider hunting in the dusty windowsill darted into the cracked wood before Barney could crush it.

"Barn? Barney? What are you doing out there?"

"Smoking," he said, swept the fluff onto the floor and put his foot over the charcoal, the stub of balsa wood. Ground it into the gray floorboards, planed smooth by the constant pacing of his heavy boots. The neat row of greased crescent wrenches grinned from the wall—the ratchet reaching out for the silver-toothed saw. On its own peg, he'd hung his favorite ball-peen hammer. He'd bullied the stiffness out of more than one welded joint with it, the bullet head stippling the rough metal. Thin light pushed through the filthy window put a gleam on the wooden handles, the greased teeth and heads of his tools. He stroked the handlebars of his Harley under its plastic cape, and pushed open the plywood door.

His wife stood on the back porch, hands on hips. "Come out of that shed, the game's starting. I got the trays set up."

"It's all ads anyway," he muttered, but wiped his fingers on his canvas apron, hung it up and closed the workshop door behind him. The lawn collapsed gently under his feet, grass soft as a woman's breast. The crocus spidered over the roots of the maple tree, its spears overgrown and already covered in withered flowers. The last cold snap had interrupted spring, covered the new buds in ice, sent the small migratory birds high into the trees to chitter and shuffle on frozen feet.

"Dinner's on the tray," Jo said. "Scrape your shoes and wash up."

The water from the tap was cold, but he immersed his hands in the spray anyway, working the soap around his rough knuckles, over the burn scars on the backs of his hands. Jo always insisted on routine once they got off the road, having inherited her family's love of the reliable, the predictable acts and words that held each day together. Consistency was Barney's small gift to her, a difficult habit for a man of the road. But in the long run it had paid off—brought Jo's life into balance. Her parents both had dementia, lived in an old folks' home on the other side of Milwaukee. Her younger brother was dead, struck by lightning.

He swiped an icy washcloth around his ears, inspected the cloth for soot, then squeezed it dry and draped it on the rack. She'd still complain how he smelled like smoke, how the welding fumes clung to his skin and beard. That smell had driven her wild, when they were younger, both made of flame and blazing for each other.

He changed into a clean shirt, almost ready for the rag pile, and slouched into the living room to settle into his recliner. Jo had wanted a matched set of furniture, but he'd thought that was too fancy. She'd already bullied him into painting the ceiling Willow Creek Green, stripping back the linoleum to show the original farmhouse tongue-and-groove. White shutters, billowing drapes: fussy things they'd laughed at when they were younger. They'd never needed these decorations. They'd lived hard, slept under the summer stars with his saddlebags for a pillow. But he had to admit it was good, now, to have a comfortable chair under a roof they'd paid for with honest money. They weren't kids anymore, Jo reminded him. It was alright to want a night's sleep in a soft bed.

On the screen—the size of a cereal box, Jo wouldn't let him get a big TV—the first quarter happened fast, Lakers moving the ball quickly over the whole court, Suns stumbling to keep up. Barney broke the crust on his microwave pot pie, let the steam wash over his face, warming the tip of his nose.

"Look at that," Jo mumbled around a mouthful of chicken. "Foul. That was a foul."

"They won't call it," Barney said. "It's still the first quarter, nobody calls fouls that early."

"Ought to learn how to play like grown men."

They rooted for the Suns because they hated the Lakers' showiness, with their celebrities cluttering the first two rows of seats. Stephen Tyler and his full-lipped daughter. Meg Ryan in a heavy coat. There was a close-up on Jack Nicholson, sitting next to a plushy redhead.

"Looks like the Devil himself," Jo said. The redhead smiled wide, realizing she was on the Tele-Monitor. She clapped with her hands high over her head, her cleavage distorting the letters on her t-shirt. Nicholson put his hand on her knee. He was wearing sunglasses and a Lakers cap, his face a mass of leering wrinkles.

"He looks the same as he did twenty years ago."

"Botox," Jo said. "Shots of formaldehyde."

They'd left LA in the early 80s, when things were getting out of control. Cocaine, cut with cheap crank had fueled the gang's wild midnight rides. They'd kidnapped a girl from a college campus, left muddy scars in the pristine turf.

Jo kept a scrapbook from that period, Polaroids and faded snapshots of their old friends in their leathers. The stolen girl, naked and wrapped in an American flag at her biker wedding. Her pale naked thighs, staring at the camera like a deer. Ripe for the taking, and they'd taken her. Everyone smiling, hoisting cans of beer. Barney and his welding crew, holding their torches up like avenging angels. Jo on her brother's Harley, shredded hot pants riding up her tan thighs. They'd been wild then, playing cowboys and Indians up and down Highway 101. Running from the police, always looking for the next big rush, the next ride. Most of the people in that album were dead now. But not thrown from a bike, peeled bloody by the asphalt. They did not have noble deaths—they died of overdoses, organs ruptured in bar fights. They hadn't known when to get out. When enough was enough.

"Too bad Shaq isn't playing this season."

"He's too old. And that Kobe Bryant, he's a diva. Doesn't want to share the court."

"What a bastard."

There was vanilla ice cream for dessert. Jo got up at halftime and scooped it into the blue bowls. She ate it straight out of the carton, too. He'd caught her before, two heaping bowls of melting vanilla on the counter and eating it out of the carton, her mouth all smeared with cream and sugar. It drove him wild, tasting that on her lips, sweeter than any flower.

"Thank you, Josephine," he said solemnly. This time, too, she had a white streak over her upper lip, like a trace of glue on the edge of a paper. She balanced her ice cream on her pillowy stomach and leaned back in her recliner.

"You're welcome, Barnes and Noble," she replied, digging her spoon deep into the dessert. He would have liked to dig his hands into her like soft sand, taste her, roll her across the rag rug while the Suns limped into the third quarter. She was 55 and he still loved the way she looked. He loved the collapsing skin under her chin, soft as silk. The way her hair always smelled of campfires for some reason.

"No sprinkles?" he joked. "No maraschino cherry?"

She rolled her eyes. "There's some Lysol under the sink."

"My favorite."

The Lakers won, of course, their money and fame and showboating overwhelming Phoenix in the fourth quarter. Jo and Barney booed the yellow-and-purple jerseys, then switched off the set when the after-game commentary started.

"You want to watch something else?" Barney asked. "Movie?"

She skimmed the bowl with her finger, licked it. "No, I'm done." The TV hummed on its plywood stand, its screen still zinging with static.

"Can I get you a magazine or something?"

"I thought I'd call my parents. It's their anniversary."

Barney thought You gonna remind them? but said nothing. She was sensitive about her parents, protected them in their decline like she never had before they'd gotten sick. She visited twice a month, knew their nurses by name. As a girl, she'd climbed out the windows of their suburban split-level, into waiting cars full of boys and beer. She'd been a Valkyrie, a wild woman swinging a chain, never losing a fight. She'd raised some hell. Not that her parents remembered.

"How many years is it now?"

"Almost 60. I don't know how many exactly. I'll make the call in the bedroom, in case you want to watch the news or something."

"You sure? You're not gonna bother me."

She put her hand on his bicep, above the faded rose with her name tattooed on it. "Babe," she said. "I'll be in the back. Come check on me in fifteen, OK?"

She put the ice cream bowls in the sink. Barney heard her lift the phone from its cradle, her finger clicking against the buttons. Then she closed the bedroom door, and her voice was muffled. Barney leaned his head back against the sofa cushions, listened to his stomach move around, the house seeming to breathe softly, belling in and out like a set of lungs. He picked up the remote control, pointed it at the set, thumbed the red Power button. The news was on now, the jagged red line of the economy stabbing lower and lower on the screen, and on another channel that new reality show about the chop shop in New Jersey. He liked that one, even though he regarded the all men who ran it as fags. Always posturing to each other, trying to be big for the cameras. Barney supposed it only made sense that men were different now than they had been twenty years ago. But it sickened him to see those shiny-clean machines being tended by such gutless morons.

He held the remote out. The plastic curved perfectly to the shape of his palm, the batteries slightly warm in their casing. The buttons were rubbery, the numbers on several of them worn away to bald spots. He pressed them in order without turning on the TV, then in diagonal and square lines. He felt a burst of heat in his legs, the cushion under him warmed as though by a breath.

He eased out of the chair and went down the hallway—Saffron Risotto paint—to unzip over the toilet. When he was finished he shook himself off and checked the sterling silver clock on the bathroom shelf.

"Jo?" He tapped gently at the bedroom door. "You've been in there for fifteen minutes. Can I come in?"

There was no answer. He put his palm on the door, trying to sense her mood through the layer of wood. Two deep breaths, and he said her name again.

"Yes," she said, voice muffled. "I'm off the phone."

She was on her back in the middle of their bed, her hands folded over her stomach. The flowered pillows crowded against her shoulders. He felt a chill in his guts—for a moment, she seemed lifeless, a body going cold by the side of the road. He was relieved to see her chest rising and falling, and when he took her hand, it was warm. Her fingers curled around his, her pulse strong against his skin. Barney sat next to her on his side of the bed. The mattress sagged under his weight, the headboard he'd welded himself clanking lightly against the wall, embellished with wrought-iron roses. He ran his hand over the knots of the chenille bedspread.

"Everything OK?"

"No." Her pale cheeks, her mascara puddling under her eyes. "It was just my mom I talked to, Dad couldn't come to the phone."

Jo squeezed her eyes shut, pressed her lips together as though to hold something steady in herself. "We talked for a couple minutes about how she and Dad are doing. The nurses, the food. Then," she said. A sob bubbled out of her. She clamped her lips together again, her body starting to shake.

"Then she asked me why I kept calling. She said they'd already paid their back taxes, and that the IRS had better stop harassing them. She screamed at me."

"She thought you were from the IRS?"

She waved her hands in the air over her stomach. "It was fine at first. She was lucid, remembered who I was. I said Happy Anniversary from both of us."

"She knew who I was, too?"

"I don't know. Sometimes she fakes it, I'm pretty sure. The way she talks."

He patted her shoulder, hoping she would turn towards him. Her face was crumpled as an old grease rag. The thick knuckles studded with silver rings clattered on her hands.

"Dad wouldn't talk to me because he's afraid of the phone. He thinks it's a Nazi thing. He told one of the nurses that it would suck his soul out his ears."

"Jesus." He touched her again. Her shoulders were thick now, rounded from sitting in comfortable chairs, bending over the stove. She wore cardigans, her reading glasses dangled from a hand-beaded chain. Some days these changes seemed ordinary enough. And other times, he woke up in the body of an aging man. How had they gotten so old? Though he didn't regret a single day he'd spent with her, the time passing as their bodies softened against each other like a pair of leather boots left in the rain.

She opened her eyes, peered at him. "It's so sad. The way they are now."

"I know it's hard."

"It's just a matter of time. I'll call or visit and she'll think I'm a stranger." She ran her hands over her face, as if smoothing the wrinkles on a bed sheet. "Didn't Jack Nicholson look awful tonight?"

"We'll look awful one day, too."

"Not like that! Like the Devil himself, truly."

Barney made them tea in the kitchen, leaning against the counter while they waited for the electric kettle to boil. Jo sat in the cane chair by the breakfast table, both of them sanded down but not yet repainted. She absentmindedly took her glasses off their chain and folded the plastic arms, arranging them by the sugar bowl. She stared into the table top as though into a mirror.

"You want something to eat? Some toast?"

"No, Barn. You always burn it, anyway."

He chuckled. "My only flaw, right?"

She wanted peppermint, so he dropped the green teabag into the water and watched the fine yellow pigments collect in the bottom of the cup. No sugar, no milk. He put the cup on her favorite saucer, the one with the violets and the chipped edge. Had it been warmer they might have sat out on the porch, resting their old bones, Jo called it. I'm just going to rest my old bones. But tonight the chill was coming out of the soil, creeping though the floorboards of the house, rattling the trickle of water in the rainspout. It was better to curl up under Jo's crocheted blankets and put on Casablanca, ignoring the all-absorbing blackness outside the windows. Spring, everywhere, stretched out its green claws—the start of leaf and blade—rending open the earth.

It had been spring when they'd kidnapped that redhaired girl, almost thirty years ago. A men-only ride, Jo and the women were left to terrorize one another in the house they all shared. Barney leaned over the sink, a cold splash of air from the drain catching his whiskers. He'd been the one who caught her—the UCLA sweatshirt tied over her shoulders, a younger guy trying feebly to help her as Barney tore her away. She hadn't stopped screaming until Barney got her pants off, in the red circle of firelight with his friends' faces in a ring above them. Twenty years later, it was harder for him to conjure the girl's face, the details of that night slipping away. The aluminum taste of her split lip, the golden patch of hair. The way he laughed at the blood, disbelieving, when she whispered, it's my first time, please be gentle. Poured pissy beer into her contorting mouth as the others took their turns. They called it a wedding.

Jo never knew about it—initiation was men's business. If she'd guessed what he'd done, she hadn't said anything. At the after party, spinning with cocaine, Jo had braided the girl's red hair, wrapped the American flag around her like a bridal veil. Can we keep her as a pet? she'd asked, crying when they left the girl at the crossroads. She hadn't seen the bruises on the girl's arms, the marks left on her. He'd never told Jo about that redheaded girl. He'd sensed that even Jo would not forgive him, if she'd known. A virgin. Of course they couldn't keep her, after that.

Barney was blessed, in a way, by Jo's willingness to look the other way. And somehow that made life bearable. The memory was his alone, a rough, salty nugget to roll over in these sweet days—as sharp as a stone in his shoe. A reminder of his old wickedness to keep his heart warm.

"Do you still want to drive over on Monday? I'm not working," Barney offered. He'd put too much water in his tea, and could barely taste the chamomile. It smelled like bathroom potpourri. "I might even get out the bike, if it's not raining."

Jo sighed. "Yeah, we should go. You never know, right?"

"I'll still love you when we're old and crazy. We'll terrorize the candy stripers together."

"We'll keep our savings in a coffee can," Jo said. She smiled weakly. "You can ride your Harley all up and down the nursing home halls."

He leaned back, smiling to the ceiling. The words felt like the beginnings of prayers. "Sounds like our wild youth."

"A million years ago," she said.

In the movie, Ingrid Bergman's love letter bled with rain. They already knew what it said, by heart, nearly as well as they knew Bogart's look of bitter disappointment. Jo took Barney's hand, touched the scorched place in his beard.

"Barn," she asked in lazy wonderment, "You been setting yourself on fire again?"

"It's a bad habit," he said, putting his hand over hers. "Silly to think you wouldn't notice."

Doll

Cyndee liked him to leave the windows open in the summer. After sex, she lay back against the pillows, a cigarette already flickering at her lips. The light was kind to her—in daylight, Tony thought, she looked hard, mean. Across the street, a CD player propped in someone's window pumped out music, loud and dirty. A car pulled up, spray-painted a flat orange and buffed to a dull shine.

"You going somewhere?" she asked him. He fumbled for his boxers. He could hear a whining somewhere in the room. The music across the street changed to a quick crunk, loosening something in his head like a broken filament. Friday night.

"Maybe you should," Cyndee said, and crushed out her cigarette on the wooden crate they used for a bedside table.

"What?"

Her eyes slitted. "Antwone's coming over to pick me up, and I'd rather you not be here."

"You broke up with Antwone."

"Well, now he's coming over. He's taking me out." Her acrylic nails clicked on the crate beside her. She was losing patience with him already, and he hadn't even tried to make her explain. He slapped at his arm, sure he felt a mosquito landing there.

Tony slid his legs off the bed and felt around on the floor for his pants.

"I'm not going to ask why," he said. He wanted to smack her. "I'm not going to say what I'm feeling."

"Fine," she said. "I won't ask, then. Nobody's going to ask anybody anything."

‡

He got dressed in silence, shoving his feet into his Nikes so hard that his socks jammed around his ankles. He wasn't sure if Cyndee was watching him, but he avoided her eyes anyway. She was always jabbing at him, he thought. She intentionally did cruel things, just to see what he'd do. Sometimes, she'd get him really angry—once he'd come home and a pack of strangers were sitting in their living room, drinking his beer and leaving ash on the carpet. She'd looked at him and smiled, tipping up her drink, another man's hand creeping up her thick thigh. *Pussy*, she mouthed at him, her eyes thin as pencil lines. She gave out her phone number to strangers.

‡

He was a pussy. Even when Cyndee was at her most cruel, he'd never taken steps to get her back in line. The neighbors in the next apartment over regularly, on the other hand, had screaming fights, punctuated by the sounds of ashtrays or remote controls or thick plates hitting the walls. The woman in this couple sometimes had a fat lip. Occasionally, she limped when she walked across the parking area to do her load of coin-op laundry. Cyndee hated this woman, straight up despised her.

"You'd never catch me getting beat on by some dumb motherfucker," she'd say, sitting in judgment on the porch. Her cigarette crisped down to the filter, but she put it to her lips again and again, looking at the neighbor woman's ashy knees. "Pathetic."

Tony thought of this neighbor woman as he grabbed his keys from the crate on his side of the bed. She looked like someone Tony knew from high school, another beaten-looking girl who dated one wannabe thug after another. He touched his lower lip on his way out the bedroom. He didn't bother to say goodbye to Cyndee. He could feel the weight of her eyes on his back, her teeth snipping at him in a mean smile. *Pussy*.

The night was warm but losing its humidity, like a body fading into sleep. Tony called his friend Jamal on his cell phone. Jamal was at Washington's, the dive down the street. Jamal thought it was tacky to drink at home, and he preferred the salt-dusty peanuts and two-dollar pitchers he could get in the bar.

"What that bitch do now?" Jamal asked. In the background, Tony could hear the jukebox turned up loud, playing some overdubbed hip-hop. "You should come by, man. I'm thinking I'm going out tonight, you could go with me. Cool?"

"A'ight," Tony said. He clicked his cell phone shut and stuck his hands in his belt. The apartment complex across the street was fully lit now. Every unit had a couple by its door everybody smoking in their lawn chairs. A few folks had wrapped Christmas lights through the balcony handrails, and somebody on the first floor had Dre turned up as loud as he would go. Tony caught a whiff of powerful skunk weed as he walked the blocks to Washington's.

Jamal wanted to go out, he'd said. Going out meant something different, something to let off some steam—smoke—kick back for a change. Jamal worked for the post office, so he knew the strange parts of the city better than most. It didn't hurt that he hated Cyndee. Tony pushed his shoulders back, trying to open his chest into a confidence he didn't quite feel. Tonight could be good. It could be what he needed.

†

At Washington's, the jukebox was pumping out the weak-ass remixes, and all the pool tables were taken, so they didn't stay except to pay Jamal's tab and tip the bartender. Jamal had parked nearby, so they walked to his car. Jamal was buzzing and optimistic. He punched Tony in the shoulder, hopping around like a prizefighter. He was about eight inches shorter than Tony, thick in the middle. He stuck a cinnamon stick behind his ear, to help him quit smoking, or else attract women.

"Man, fuck that bitch," Jamal said. "You shouldn't be dating her anyway."

"I know," Tony said. He thought of Antwone, slipping into the hollow on his side of the bed. He thought of Cyndee's mean smile softening, sweetening in a rare way. "Fuck it, man. Let's go out."

"Go out! Go *out*! Too bad I'm broke, or we could go to a titty bar."

"Too bad," Tony said. He hated titty bars anyway. Cyndee had been working at a strip club when he'd met her. The manager had fired her for stealing the other girls' tips from the lockers in their break room. Cyndee said that he'd never been able to prove it, but she'd stopped stripping at the clubs in that part of town.

Jamal tapped a fist on his shoulder again. "What's better than a titty bar?"

"Robbing a bank," Tony said. He was half-joking. Jamal had gone to court for helping a friend boost a few cars, and the year before Tony himself had almost been caught with a sixteen-year-old girl behind the bleachers of the high school. He knew Jamal loved to take things—they both loved to go where they weren't wanted.

"Close, man, close. Tonight, we gonna bust open UPS."

They both laughed. Jamal hated UPS, which, Tony supposed, was part of working for the regular post office. You had your team, and you stuck with them and hated on the competition.

"I got a way in," Jamal said. "I got a way in, and I swear, son, we are *going out* tonight. You are gonna get that bitch out yo' system, and we are going *out*."

‡

They got into Jamal's ride, a 1980s Lincoln with faded, stained upholstery. Jamal had forgotten to wash it for Friday, so the paint job was riddled with dry pigeon turds. But there was a little bit of weed in the dash, and a good stereo system, so they hotboxed the car to some Big L and set off cruising towards the UPS building. Jamal rolled down all the windows.

"This gon' be easy, man," he said. The weed was lighting up Tony's stomach, adding an orange glow to the streetlights.

"Oh yeah?" Tony said. He felt himself loosening. The backs of his legs started to twitch involuntarily—something that happened every time he smoked. Big L's bass line worked its way out of the speakers and across his ankles.

"Yep, got a key and everything. This is kid stuff. But I thought it would be good to look around, you know, see what the other guy's doin' these days." Jamal laughed. He tipped his head back, looking like a rooster, and laughed again, stiff as a cartoon character. His laughter thudded on the cardboard in Tony's head. *Ha. Ha. Ha.* For a minute, Tony doubted that Jamal was a real person. He was tempted to grab the wheel and spin them across the blacktop. Nothing could hurt them—Jamal's face was a rubbery mask, grinning wide enough to swallow a grapefruit.

"You OK, man?" Jamal said to Tony. "You look kind of fucked up."

"Yeah," said Tony. He pushed his fingers into the corners of his eyes. "This is some good weed."

"Yeah it is. I found it in one of my express delivery packages. Somebody was shipping it in a pound of coffee, but I could smell it through the bag. I ripped that shit open and pow! There it was. All for me and all for free." He laughed again and drummed his palms on the steering wheel. "Here we are, man."

He pulled up beside a flowering cherry tree, its petals long gone with the spring. The Lincoln's tires rubbed against the curb. The UPS building across the street was dull-looking, the sandy brown of a Betty Crocker box cake. Jamal fished a key out of his pocket.

"Took it off a sucker on his lunch break," he said. The key twisted and shone like an anchovy between his fingers. "You cool, man? You ready to go?"

"I'm ready," Tony said. "Do we need to do the plates?" Sometimes, if they thought there were security cameras, they'd carefully unscrew Jamal's license plates and stash them on the floor behind the driver's seat.

"I don't think so." Jamal stuck his head out the window and peered at the building across the street. "I don't see any cameras. And anyway, we parked in the dark."

They got out slowly. Tony rolled his shoulders. He felt a mosquito land on his hand and whisked it away without slapping. This was the beginning of the good part—the part where, like children, they'd ease the car doors shut, holding the latches until the last minute. They'd speak in whispers. They left their cell phones turned off and sealed in the glove box, beside the baggie of weed. Jamal hopped on one foot.

"Man, this is the shit!" he stage-whispered to Tony. Tony nodded, smiled.

He sidestepped a pile of broken glass, the shards of somebody's High Life.

It was good to have a key, a pleasant change from their usual crude methods: crowbar, hammer, screwdriver. Jamal opened the door and lifted the handle, hard. That was supposed to knock off any squeaking. An air-conditioned wave of air hit them as they went inside. The ceilings were higher than Tony had thought, and the place was jammed with metal shelves. Each shelf was covered in packages.

"Merry Christmas," Jamal said. He pulled out a pocketknife. "Take your pick, man, we got all night." He walked down the first row of shelves, humming *O Holy Night*. He stuck the knife into a big, brown-paper box. The paper tore with a sigh. Jamal giggled. He rocked the knife back and forth, widening the cut.

Tony wandered through the aisles. His shoes scuffed slightly on the concrete floor. The night lights were on—every sixth fluorescent tube flitted in its casing, giving the room a greenish cast. He patted his fingers on a few of the boxes, liking the dry sound of his flesh on the paper wrappings. He could hear Jamal a few aisles over, slitting open another package. It was like being in a game show, one of the ones where you were handed a prize but you didn't know what it was—and you had to choose if you wanted to keep it or trade it for something known, like a maple-fiberboard bedroom set. If they felt like it, Jamal and Tony could be here all night, unwrapping one package at a time. They could make a pile of crumpled paper, and another one of presents, high as the flickering green lights.

Tony sucked the air between his teeth. He could get something for Cyndee; maybe one of these packages had a teddy bear or a bracelet or something she'd like. He thought of her skin, dimpled with cellulite and marred in places by black tattoos. She had some guy's name on the back of her shoulder. When they did it doggy-style, which Tony didn't particularly like but Cyndee did, he was careful to put his palm over this other man's name. It was foolish, but he didn't like to think that she'd been with anyone else. He tapped on a few boxes with his fingernails, as if testing a melon for ripeness. Jamal was still cruising through his own aisle, now singing louder. *Good King Wenceslas looked out! On the feast of Stephen!* Tony's breath was coming in shallow. The weed was taking hold of him, dragging him by the hair into a black-and-white tunnel where every sound echoed loudly in his head.

Towards the back wall, the packages started to pile up. These were the boxes that were too big for the shelves: the ones shaped like cellos, the ones the size of refrigerators. Tony gave a few of them experimental kicks. If there was a set of bedside tables, he could bring them home. Cyndee would like that. She hated the little crates they had by their mattress. *Brightly shone the moon that night! Though the frost was croo-el!* His foot knocked against a high, narrow box. It sounded hollow. There were big, hand-lettered warnings written all over it that said THIS END UP and FRAGILE. The paper was meticulously taped around the corners. Tony put his ear to the side of the package, listening. The package was silent.

"What'up, man, you find something or what?" Jamal came up behind him, clicking his pocketknife shut. Tony jumped a little, but he didn't want to show it so he sat down on the floor instead. Jamal's eyes were yellow and bleary. He squinted at Tony's box.

"Some people are so picky," he said. "Look at all that." He traced the curve of the word CAREFUL with his finger.

"This is the one I want," Tony said. The floor was cool against his legs. Looking up at Jamal made his eyelids feel heavy, so he closed them one at a time to give them a rest. Maybe the box held a huge painting in a heavy frame, a naked woman riding a tiger or something. Maybe it was a million-dollar piece of art. Even a bedroom set would be pretty exciting.

"Go to it, man," Jamal said, and flipped the pocketknife into Tony's lap. Tony unfolded the blade and started to slip it between the tape and the brown paper. He lifted the two apart slowly.

"Just stab it," Jamal said. "Stab that UPS fucker, it feels better." But Tony went along slowly, peeling down the wrapping in sheets. It he didn't like what he found, he wanted to be able to put it back the way it was.

"You find anything good?" he asked Jamal. It was good to keep Jamal talking; when Jamal was stoned he got bored quickly and didn't want to take time doing anything. Jamal pulled a handful of glittering chains out of his pocket.

"Check this shit out," he said. He shook his fist, making the jewelry shimmer. "I hit the jackpot, huh? There was a whole box of this shit."

"Damn," Tony said. He'd worked his way around to the third side of the box. Cyndee would like one of those, he thought. Then he remembered that Cyndee was out with her ex-boyfriend Antwone—in all likelihood, they had probably had a few drinks and gone back to his place. They might be screwing each other at that very moment. He slipped the knife through the last strip of masking tape.

"It's probably nothing," Jamal said. "We get boxes like this a lot at my place. Usually they just baby toys or decorations for people's gardens. You might have a light-up crèche in there or something." He opened his hand and stared at the jewelry, picking out one strand at a time.

Tony pushed the paper aside on the floor. The box was about as high as his chest, and big enough that he couldn't have gotten his arms around it.

"Look at this," he said, and kicked the box with his toe.

"Holy shit," Jamal said, looking.

‡

The box had a doorknob drawn on it in crayon. Tony stepped back from where he'd been squatting. The pocketknife dangled in his fingers. One of the lights overhead started to flicker, and his senses told him it was getting ready to pop. He heard helicopter blades and it took him a minute to realize that it was his pulse, whooshing through his temples.

"I don't know if you should open this," Jamal said. Jamal's eyes were clotted with the weed. He looked at Tony, and Tony saw that one of the tiny veins in Jamal's eyes had burst. The spot was the color of a supermarket rose petal. Tony tried not to stare at it.

"What do you think it is?" Tony said. "Don't give me any vampire shit. It's not alive. There aren't any air holes."

"I don't know, man, it's just fucking creepy." Jamal put one of his stolen necklaces between his lips and started to chew on it in a distracted way. "It's like a movie or something."

Tony knelt beside the box. The hairs on his legs stood up from the chill of the floor. Jamal started to bounce on his feet, shuffling like a boxer.

"Be cool, man, I just want to see what it is." Tony slit open the side of the box lengthwise, cutting a door in the cardboard. "You're making me nervous, Jamal."

"Can't help it," Jamal said. "You sure it's not alive?"

"No air holes," Tony said, and pulled open the box. The overhead lights, sickly green, gave a shadow to the thing inside. Jamal screamed, a strangled noise that stalled out in his throat. There was a woman's body in the box, tied to an aluminum lawn chair with gardening twine. Tony jumped back. The woman's hair was high and ratty, and her eyes stared at the floor, fixed as a doll's.

"Run," Jamal said, and took two fast steps backwards. He kept looking at the woman, his bloodshot eye wide and scared. He grabbed Tony's shoulder. "She's dead, man, run!"

But Tony looked carefully, and he couldn't see any blood. The woman's neck, shadowed by her black hair, was unbruised. He pushed Jamal's hand away. He stepped forward and stooped down, reaching into the box. He touched the woman's cheek, as he'd been taught in his high school CPR class.

"Miss, are you OK? Are you OK?" Her skin was perfectly smooth, and exactly the same temperature as the room. Tony saw that her hair was synthetic. Her nails, sloppily painted, lay stiffly on the lawn chair's arms. Tony took hold of her fingers and squeezed them.

"She's not real," he said. He turned and looked over his shoulder. Jamal was hopping from one foot to the other. The stolen jewelry, forgotten, clinked in his fist. "She's not real, dude. It's a doll."

"No way."

"Come and look, motherfucker," Tony said. He grabbed the doll's chair and pulled it forward into the light. "See? Not real."

Jamal bent down and stared at the doll's face. He licked his finger and reaching between her outrageously long eyelashes, gently touched her left eyeball. When she didn't blink, he tried to pinch her cheek, but he couldn't get a grip on her plastic skin.

"Man, that is freaky!" Jamal started to laugh. "I thought she was dead!" They stood back together and regarded the doll. Her head sagged forward so that her hair touched her lap. She was dressed in the plain clothes of a receptionist: button-down shirt, slacks, and flat shoes. Tony saw how one of her feet was slightly pigeon-toed, as if in a gesture of shyness.

"You gotta help me lift her," he said to Jamal. "I can't carry the chair by myself."

"Are you crazy? You're putting her back in her box and that's it," Jamal said. He stuck the jewelry in his pocket and left his hand there, clenching and unclenching it. Tony knew that he did this when he wasn't sure about something.

"Come on, Jamal," Tony said. He watched Jamal's hand flexing in his pocket. "This is what I'm taking. My Christmas present."

Jamal's hand kept up its steady, nervous work.

"It would really fuck things up for those UPS guys," Tony said, and he knew he'd said the right thing because Jamal pulled his hands out of his pockets.

"Let's move this thing," he said, and grabbed the lawn chair. Tony grabbed it too and they lifted the doll like a queen and carried her out to the street. By the car, Tony had to cut the doll's ties with Jamal's pocketknife so they could put her in the backseat. He decided that the Lincoln's trunk was not big enough to accommodate her.

"Are you kidding?" Jamal said when Tony opened the rear passenger door. "I could fit three bodies in there. Just put her in the trunk."

Tony lifted the doll and slid her onto the car's faded upholstery. She was lying on her side, with her back against the seats. One hand flopped onto the floor by the empty McDonald's wrappers and beer cans. Without thinking, Tony lifted it and tucked it under her head. The doll seemed to wear a faint smile, although her eyes stayed fixed.

‡

Jamal made him roll another joint while they drove away. He drummed his palms on the steering wheel. "This is the weirdest shit I've ever done," he said. "If we get pulled over we are so busted."

"Why? Nobody can prove she's not ours."

"She? You mean it. It doesn't look like a doll, man. It looks like two brothers just kidnapped a white woman tied to a chair and stuck her in the back of their car."

"She's not white white," Tony said. He turned to look behind them, the joint crackling between his fingers. The doll looked back at him. He could see down her shirt. "She looks kind of Egyptian. Greek maybe."

"You're crazy."

"Whatever, Jamal."

"You know what it is, right?" Jamal asked. He took the joint from Tony and puffed at it. "Roll the window down. That is not a toy for children. That is a sex doll. That is some dude's fuck-toy."

Tony turned around again. He stared into the backseat. The doll had big, pointy breasts and her mouth looked malleable, soft. Her eyelashes were so thick that she looked like a cartoon. Tony thought of her fingernail polish, so sloppily applied, and he saw a man holding her hand, painting each nail with clumsy strokes.

"I'm serious, man. Let's pull over and look at its pussy. Just pull the pants down."

"No way," he said to Jamal. "Tha's nasty."

"That's what that thing is for," Jamal said. He turned up the stereo, which meant the conversation was over. "Hate to be the one to tell you."

‡

Jamal drove Tony back to his apartment building with Big L bumping in the blown-out speakers. The light in Tony's apartment was off. Cyndee was still out, and part of Tony felt relief at the dark windows. Maybe she'd decide that she wanted to be with somebody else permanently. Maybe she'd move out on her own.

"Tony," Jamal said. "What are you going to do with your Christmas present?"

"I don't know." Tony pressed his knuckles against his lips, which helped him think better.

"So you know, I'm not helping you carry it up the stairs, stick it in your closet. People be thinking I'm crazy too." Jamal peeked into the backseat. "I got a blanket you could wrap it in, though."

"Thanks."

They wrapped the doll in a ratty Army surplus blanket that Jamal had in the trunk. Tony tried to be careful and tuck the blanket around the doll, but her arms kept flopping out. Jamal grabbed it from him. "Man, quit being such a bitch. It ain't gonna get mad at you." He yanked on the doll a few times. "There. Perfect."

Tony lifted the bundle onto his shoulder. The doll draped over his arm, bending at her waist. He felt like a comic-book caveman, dragging a woman off to his den. The doll's hair hung out one end of the blanket, but there was nothing they could do about that. Jamal offered Tony a plastic garbage bag, but Tony wouldn't take it.

"It can't breathe, man," Jamal said, but he shrugged and put the bag back in his trunk. His pager had lit up with some girl's number, and he was eager to leave.

"Have a good night," Tony said as Jamal started the Lincoln. He didn't watch the car pull away, and he didn't stop to check out the action at the complex across the street. He heard the neighbors' twinkling hip-hop music as he carried the doll up the stairs to his apartment. She swayed against him, her head knocking gently into his knees. He had to open the lock with one hand so that he wouldn't have to put her down by the door, like a sack of groceries.

‡

"Here we are," he said as he stepped onto the dingy living room carpet. The place stunk of Cyndee's cigarettes. There was the hamster-cage smell of the garbage, which he hadn't taken out. He went to the bedroom, the doll hanging from him. He paused at the door, listening.

It was silent. Tony nudged the door open with his foot. He snapped on the lamp by the bed. Cyndee had left the bedroom window all the way open, letting the mosquitoes in. Tony laid the doll across the bed and closed the window. Then he pushed the blanket open and sat on the bed, looking at the doll.

"You're a quiet one," he said, joking. The doll stared at the ceiling. Tony couldn't tell if she was smiling or not; her face looked different than it had in the car. He pushed a few stray hairs off her face. She was a pale, pale brown, with brown eyes that turned up at the edges. She looked like a picture of Cleopatra that Tony had seen once in an art book. Her mouth wore the pinkish traces of old lipstick at its joints. Tony lifted a finger to her lips but didn't touch her. He let his finger hover over her mouth. He halfway expected to feel her breathing, but she didn't move. Her eyes stayed on the broken ceiling fan. Cyndee, in an artistic mood, had draped the fan blades with Mardi Gras beads and cheap cloth flowers.

"Cyndee might not be coming back tonight," Tony said. He looked at the thick brush of the doll's eyelashes. "You wouldn't like Cyndee. She's pretty cold to women." He took a quick, shallow breath and—just for a second— pressed the pad of his finger to the doll's lips. Suddenly he felt that the two of them were playing Truth Or Dare at a sleepover party. The weed swirled briefly in his brain, making him laugh at himself.

"What's that name? Nefertiti? You look like Nefertiti." His voice sounded flat against the stained brown carpet, the Christmas cactus withering in the corner. For a moment he wasn't sure if he spoke out loud or if it was only his brain, turned all the way up. Tony laughed again, a dry cough that made him swallow hard on his own tongue.

"So where you from, Nefertiti? What's your horoscope?" He took the doll's hand and turned it over. Her palm was smooth, with a few generic-looking creases to show where her plastic bones were. Tony ran his fingers over those three creases, smiling. "You want me to read your future?" He'd seen other men in bars use these lines on real women, beauties with coils of braids piled high on their heads. The women, drinking their beers through multicolored straws so they wouldn't mess up their lipliner, had laughed, acquiescing. They had extended their hands to be held and kissed, stroked by the fingers of hopeful strangers. The doll watched Tony as he pondered her life line.

"Oh, you'll live a long time," he said, teasing. "You're going to be one of those old grandmas who sit on the porch all day. Sitting in the sun." He pretended to feel the doll's palm. "Maybe you'll have a long journey, go back to Egypt. Nefertiti's an Egyptian name, right? Can I call you Tita?" He smiled at the doll, and her eyes looked into his. She waited for him to go on.

"Okay, so a long journey. And you'll meet a dark and handsome stranger right—here," he said, and kissed the spot on her hand. He giggled, as he imagined Tita would giggle, too. Her eyes turned up at the corners in a delicate smile, making Tony suddenly shy.

He let go of her hand and scooted off the bed.

"You wanna beer?" he asked, already nodding at his own question. There were clean glasses and even a straw in the kitchen. He got two beers out of the crisper and poured them out with his usual care. Cyndee used to make fun of him for his fussiness, but he felt that Tita would appreciate it. The beers had almost no head, just a little rim of foam that clung to the edge of the glass. He put a straw in one of them and carried them back into the bedroom.

"Where were we?" he asked. He was starting to get the little migraine he always got when he smoked weed. It made his forehead pucker, as if some tiny muscle was pulling his eyeballs backwards into his head. He took a few quick swallows of his beer, hoping to hold it off. "That's right. You gonna meet a handsome prince." He put his hand into Tita's hand, which lay softly on the bed.

"Someday my prince will come," he sang in a falsetto. He had grown up on Disney cartoons and knew all the songs by heart. "That's what I'm talking about. Your dark and handsome man." He had a few more gulps of beer. Tita's glass sat untouched on one of the crates by the bed, its straw swaying back and forth in the slight breeze from the open window. Tony was tempted to hold the straw to her lips, but he was in no hurry. He squeezed her fingers.

"Now do me," he said, turning his hand palm-up on the bed. "Tell me what's going to happen." Tita's fingers cradled his hand, tickling the fine hairs that grew on his skin. Tony closed his eyes and breathed in, and the whole world shrank to their two hands brushing against one another. He smiled and reached for her cheek. It was smooth and warm under his touch. His thumb groped across her full lower lip, and her mouth opened very slightly to accommodate him.

"You're so pretty," he said. He looked at her again. "I can tell even with my eyes closed." He put down his beer and reached for her hair with the other hand. It was heavy and tangled; he could tell she hadn't had it styled in a long time. He smoothed it away from her face and gently tucked it back. He felt a thin seam in the plastic behind her ear.

"I'm so glad I found you," Tony said. He held her face, looking into her eyes. "I feel like it's fate or something. I mean, I could have opened any box." Tita smiled at him.

"Let's not talk anymore," he said, and tugged the doll towards him. She didn't pull back, or resist, or tell him he was doing it wrong. She fit against his body perfectly. One of her arms fell across his waist. They lay that way on the stale sheets for a long time. He listened very hard, until the neighbors' music and laughter and the clacking cars outside faded under the sound of his anxious heartbeat. Pressed to his chest, Tita moved in time with his pulse. Her face was close and perfect. Tony looked into her glassy eyes, waiting for her sign. He could feel himself breathing, breathing, breathing for both of them.

THE AUTHOR

CLAIRE RUDY FOSTER

Claire's critically recognized short fiction appears in various respected
journals, including *McSweeney's, Vestal Review, and SmokeLong Quarterly*.
She has been honored by several small presses, including a nomination
for the Pushcart Prize. She holds an MFA in Creative Writing. She is
afraid of sharks, zombies, and other imaginary monsters. She lives in
Portland, Oregon.

ACKNOWLEDGEMENTS

This collection would not have been possible without an immense amount of support. What follows is an incomplete list names—thank you, all of you. When I could not walk, you reminded me that I can fly.

Chris Aguirre, Chris Anderson, Phil Bennett, Willie and Rene Conable, Kristi Coulter, Steph and Mike Greenough, Erica Griffin, Michael Hashizume, Bill Kenny, Kathy Mahoney, Dan Maurer, Charlie Peirson, Aaron Perry, Nik Sauter, Margaret Pinard, Becca Saunders, Paul Silva, Izarra Varela, Alan Weintraut, and all my #xa people.

I would also like to thank my family, especially my Grammie Anne, for a lifetime of encouragement, love, and help. You are my rock.

Most of all, this book is for Lewis, an excellent writer.